STUDENT EDITION

Other books by Kyle Idleman

Not a Fan

Not a Fan Student Edition

Gods at War

STUDENT EDITION

THE BATTLE FOR YOUR HEART THAT WILL DEFINE YOUR LIFE

kyle idleman
bestselling author of not a fan.

ZONDERVAN

Gods at War Student Edition
Copyright © 2014 by Kyle Idleman

This title is also available as a Zondervan ebook. Visit www.zondervan.com/ebooks.

Requests for information should be addressed to:

Zondervan, Grand Rapids, Michigan 49546

ISBN 978-0-310-74253-1

Cover design: Curt Diepenhorst and Cindy Davis
Interior design: Beth Shagene

Printed in the United States of America

14 15 16 17 18 19 20 21 22 23 24 25 /DCI/ 14 13 12 11 10 9 8 7 6 5 4 3 2 1

Thank you, Jesse Florea, for the hard work, dedication, and passion you brought to this student edition. You stepped in when needed and went above and beyond to make a very tight deadline, while also taking the time to do thorough research to find great stories and facts specifically for this book. I am pleased that the gods at war message is now in a form students will connect with, and thankful you were there to help make it a reality.

contents

introduction

With the camera rolling, an interviewer walks up to a couple of teenagers in a park.

"Name as many of the Ten Commandments as you can," he says.

The teens' eyes grow wide. "You have a right to — Oh, wait, no," one of the guys starts to say. His friend laughs. Off camera, another teen begins reciting the books of the Bible: "Genesis, Exodus, Leviticus, Numbers, Deuteronomy, Joshua …"

"You might as well put the camera on him," the other guy says, pointing to the kid who knows his Bible but is obviously confused.

After a little while, a light bulb goes off for one of the boys. "Thou shall not steal," he says, smiling. "No fornication." Another chimes in, "No sex before you get married." Then, "*Uhhh* …" Silence.

"Well, do you think you do a good job following them?" the interviewer asks.

"No, not really." No hesitation this time from the teens.

The video also asks adults and other teens about their knowledge of the Ten Commandments.

"I can name all twelve," one person says.

"Thou shalt not steal," comes up a lot.

"Thou shalt not kill."

"Thou shalt not covet another man's wife."

"Honor thy father and thy mother."

"Do not take the Lord's name in vain."

"Thou shalt not commit adultery."

"Do not give false witness against a neighbor."

In all, the people in the video manage to come up with seven of the Ten Commandments.[1]

That's not bad — much better than when Jay Leno went to the street in one of his "Jaywalking" segments.

"How many Commandments are there?" Jay asks a young woman.

"Ten." She grins.

"Can you name any of them?" Jay continues.

"Freedom of speech."

Studies have shown that most people know the ingredients of a McDonald's Big Mac better than they know the Bible's Ten Commandments. In a survey of one thousand people, eight hundred of them knew that "two all-beef patties" could be found in a Big Mac. But only six hundred knew the commandment of thou shalt not kill. And less than half of the people remembered the commandment to honor thy father and mother. Yet six out of ten people knew the Big Mac has a pickle.[2] (Maybe we just have to come up with a catchy Commandments jingle.)

Many people surveyed said they'd memorized the Ten Commandments when they were younger but couldn't remember them anymore. How about you? Can *you* name all Ten Commandments?

My eight-year-old daughter Morgan certainly can. And believe it or not, her memorization of those commandments changed my life and the life of the church where I'm a pastor. As I tucked her into bed one night, Morgan recited the greatest Top Ten list of all time, including the first two commandments that everybody seems to forget: "You shall have no other gods before me" and "You shall not make for yourself an idol."

When she finished, I smiled. "Wow," I said. Then I asked the same question as the interviewer in the video: "Do you do a good job following them?"

Morgan looked at the ground as she admitted that she'd lied and didn't always honor her father and mother.

But then her eyes became bright and she said, "Dad, I know one commandment I have never broken! I've never made an idol."

I smiled, holding my tongue. I wanted to tell my daughter that, as a matter of fact, that commandment is the very one we all break most often. But as I said good night to my young daughter, I decided to save the theology lesson for another day. We prayed and thanked God for sending Jesus to take away our sin and guilt. As I left her room, I gave her a smile and a kiss on the forehead, and told her I was proud of her for memorizing the Ten Commandments.

But walking down the steps, I wondered how many people see idolatry exactly as Morgan did. Maybe they see the Ten Commandments as a checklist, like the rules posted at the community swimming pool — no running, no diving, no peeing in the pool. Just a long list of rules. And the one about idols is quickly skipped over because they think they've got that bullet point covered.

After all, the whole subject of idolatry seems obsolete. That command was for the time of golden calves, not now. Right?

As for those thousand or so references to idolatry in the Bible, haven't they expired? We don't know anyone who kneels before golden statues or bows down before carved images. Hasn't idolatry gone the way of parachute pants, beehive hairstyles, and three layers of grungy flannel shirts? Aren't we past all that?

Idolatry seems so primitive. So irrelevant. Is a book on idolatry even necessary? Why not a book about rain dancing and MySpace? (Although Justin Timberlake may help bring that one back.)

And yet idolatry is the number one issue in the Bible. That should catch our attention. Idolatry shows up in every book. More than fifty of the laws in the Bible's first five books are aimed at this issue. In all of Judaism, it was one of only four sins that came with the death penalty attached.

Seeing my faith and life through the lens of idolatry has rebuilt my relationship with God from the ground up. As I've talked with my friends and people at church about it, they've agreed this issue is a game changer.

When we look at life through the lens of idolatry, it becomes clear that there's a war going on. The gods are at war, and their strength is not to be underestimated. These gods clash for the throne of your heart, and a lot is at stake. Everything about me, everything I do, every relationship I have, everything I hope or dream or wish to become, depends upon what god wins that war.

The deadliest war is the one most of us never realize is being fought. I understood how my eight-year-old daughter had yet to get a handle on the second commandment, but the problem is that most adults and people your age haven't done so either. I wonder how many of us are just where Morgan was, believing we can put a nice checkmark on that list and dismiss any concern over idols forever.

What if it's not about statues? What if the gods of here and now are not cosmic deities with strange names? What if they take identities that are so ordinary that we don't recognize them as "gods" at all? What if we do our "kneeling" and our "bowing" with our imaginations, our cash, our search engines, our calendars?

What if I told you that every sin you are struggling with, every discouragement you are dealing with, even the lack of purpose you're living with are because of idolatry?

part 1

gods at war

idolatry is the issue

Imagine a man who has been coughing constantly. This cough keeps him up half of the night and interrupts any conversation he has that lasts more than a minute. The cough is so unrelenting that he goes to the doctor.

The doctor runs some tests.

Lung cancer.

Now imagine the doctor knows how tough the news will be to handle. So he doesn't tell his patient about the cancer. Instead, he writes a prescription for some strong cough medicine and tells the man that he should feel better soon. The man is delighted with this prognosis. And sure enough, he sleeps much better that night. The cough syrup seems to have solved his problem.

Meanwhile, very quietly, the cancer eats away at his body. At my church, I talk to people every week who are "coughing."

Struggling.

Hurting.

Stressing.

Cheating.

Lusting.

Worrying.

Quitting.

Medicating.

Avoiding.

Searching.

They come to me and share their struggles.

They unload their frustrations.

They express their discouragement.

They display their hurts.

They confess their sins.

When I talk to people, they point to what they believe is the problem. In their minds, they've nailed it. They can't stop coughing. But here's what I've discovered: They're talking about a symptom rather than the true illness — the true issue — which is always idolatry.

CASE STUDY 1: No Big Deal

She's a young woman who grew up in our church. Her family wants me to meet and talk with her. They're concerned because she's about to move in with her boyfriend, who isn't a Christian. This ought to be a fun one.*

I call her twice and leave messages, but she doesn't return my call. The third time she picks up. She knows why I'm calling and tries to laugh it off.

"I can't believe my parents are making such a big deal out of this," she says with a nervous laugh. I can picture her rolling her eyes. In her mind this whole thing is a "mild cough" and nothing to worry about.

"Well, I appreciate your talking to me for a few minutes. But I have to ask, do you think it's possible that you've got this backward?"

"What do you mean?"

"That instead of making a big deal out of nothing, it could be that you're making nothing out of a big deal?"

More nervous laughter. "It's not a big deal," she says again.

---

*Not really.

"Do you mind my telling you why I think it is?"

She sighs deeply and proceeds to give me her prediction of all the reasons she thinks I'll produce.

I interrupt her with a question. "Have you thought about how much moving in together is going to cost you?"

"You mean the cost of the apartment?"

"No, I'm not necessarily talking about money. I mean the way your family feels about it, and the pressure you're getting from them. That's a kind of price, right?"

"Yeah, I guess it is, but that's their problem."

"And what is this going to cost your future marriage?"

"I don't even know if we're going to get married," she responds.

"I'm not necessarily talking about your getting married to him, because statistically speaking, you most likely won't."

She understands what I'm getting at, but I push it a bit further. "How much is this going to cost your future husband? What price will he have to pay for this decision?" She has to stop and consider that one.

I continue to count the ways that this decision is a big deal, because it's costing her more than she knows.

"So here's what I suggest. If you're willing to pay a price, then this must be pretty important to you. It must be a fairly big deal if you're willing to go through all of this."

I take her silence for reflection, and I finally get to my point. "When I see the sacrifices you are willing to make, and the fact that you are willing to ignore what God has to say about all this, it seems to me that you've turned this relationship into a god."

"What do you mean by that?"

"A god is what we sacrifice for and what we pursue. From where I sit, you have God on one side saying one thing, and your boyfriend on the other side saying something else. And you're choosing your boyfriend over God. The Bible calls that idolatry, and it's actually a pretty big deal."

No nervous laughter this time. "I've never thought about it like that," she says.

CASE STUDY 2: The Secret Struggle

He comes in maybe five or ten minutes late.

He had asked if we could talk for a few minutes, and I suggested meeting for coffee. But he wanted to meet someplace "a little more private." So we decided on my office. He arrives and pauses in the doorway, as if still not sure he wants to keep this appointment.

"Come on in." I smile and motion toward a seat.

He answers my smile with a very brief one. He sits, and his body language is all about reluctance. He wraps his arms around each other, lightly massaging his right elbow. He hasn't told me what this meeting is about, but I know. The conversation I'm about to have has become very familiar.

I ask him a few mundane questions about his life, where he's from, anything to break the ice and create a more relaxed setting.

When we've done that for a couple of minutes, he finally broaches his subject. I can tell it takes all the courage he can summon to release his long-held secret.

"I...um...I think I'm addicted to pornography, or something," he stammers.

He looks at his shoes.

"Okay. Well, you're not the first person to walk in here, sit in that seat, and say those words. How long has this been a struggle?"

He tells his story, starting when he was twelve years old and saw certain images with the guys. Pictures that disturbed him at first. Pictures that lodged in his mind, that wouldn't go away, that started calling to him. Pictures he can perfectly visualize all these years later. He talks about his hatred of the Internet. He describes the web as if it were his mortal enemy.

"It's so easy," he says. "Any kind of picture, any kind of video is at your fingertips. Just like that. Instant gratification, whenever you feel the slightest urge."

He speaks with the weary tones of a slave, of a prisoner who has given up on escape plans.

"What am I supposed to do," he says, "unplug the computer? I'm dependent on the Internet like everyone else. I need it for everything. Even if I just used my smartphone, I can pull up those images there. Turn on the television, and there are a million suggestions. Am I supposed to just watch the Disney Channel?"

He says he had no idea what pornography would do to his life, particularly his relationships. He seems to understand, at least to some degree, how it has changed the way he views and interacts with women.

"Thing is," he says, "you think it's just an itch. That's all. An itch. But it never goes away, and you have to scratch. Well, you have to scratch harder and deeper as time goes by. You know what I mean?"

"I know."

There is silence. I'm sure he's expecting me to give the same advice he's heard for so many years: Put a filter on your Internet browser. Find an accountability partner. Redirect your eyes. All helpful suggestions, but I know he's tried them all multiple times. Otherwise he wouldn't be sitting in front of me.

What I know is that there is an idol that must be dethroned, and until that happens he will suffer. He won't enjoy intimacy in relationships. He will struggle to have any real connection with God.

"You think what you have is a lust problem, but what you really have is a worship problem. The question you have to answer each day is, *Will I worship God or will I worship sex?*"

He doesn't verbalize it, but the expression on his face says, "I've never thought about it like that."

What Lies Beneath

Idolatry isn't just one of many sins. It's the one great sin that all others come from. So if you start scratching at whatever struggle you're dealing with, eventually you'll find a false god underneath. Until that god is dethroned, and the Lord God takes his rightful place, you will not have victory.

Idolatry isn't an issue; it is *the* issue. All roads lead to the dusty, overlooked concept of false gods. Deal with life on the glossy outer layers, and you might never see it. But scratch a little beneath the surface, and you begin to see that it's always there. There are a hundred million different symptoms, but the issue is always idolatry.

That's why, when Moses stood on Mount Sinai and received the Ten Commandments from God, the first one was, "I am the Lord your God, who brought you out of Egypt, out of the land of slavery. You shall have no other gods before me" (Exodus 20:2 – 3).

When God issued this command during the time of Moses, the people were familiar with a lot of other gods. God's people had spent more than four hundred years in Egypt as slaves. Egypt was crowded with gods. They had taken over the neighborhood — literally. The Egyptians had local gods for every district. Egypt was the Baskin-Robbins of gods. You could pick and choose the flavors you wanted.

The Bible has a different standard. When we hear God say, "You will have no other gods before me," we think of it as a hierarchy: God is always in first place. But there are no places. God isn't interested in competing against others or being first among many.

God will not be part of any hierarchy.

He wasn't saying "before me" as in "ahead of me." A better understanding of the Hebrew word translated "before me" is "in my presence."

God declines to step inside the octagon; he is the ultimate fighting champion. He is not interested in competing in a reality

TV show; he is the ultimate reality. Life doesn't work properly until every other "contestant" sitting around the boardroom of your heart is fired.

There are no partial gods, no honorary gods, no interim gods, no assistants to the regional gods.

God isn't saying this because he is insecure, but because it's the way of truth in this universe. Only one God created it. Only one God designed it, and only one God knows how it works. He is the only God who can help us, direct us, satisfy us, save us.

As the events unfold in Exodus 20, the one true God has had it with the imitation and substitute gods. So God tells the nation of Israel to break up the band of gods. Send them packing. All other god activity is cancelled. He makes sure the people understand that he is the one and only. He is the Lord God.

You may be thinking, *Thanks for the history lesson, but that was a long time ago. Today, the problem doesn't appear to be that people worship many gods; it's that they don't worship any god.*

Yet my guess is that our list of gods is longer than theirs. Just because we call them by different names doesn't change what they are. We may not have the god of knowledge, the god of agriculture, the god of sex, or the god of the hunt. But we do have GPAs, cars, pornography, and sports. If it walks like an idol, and quacks like an idol, it's probably...*

You can call it a cough instead of calling it cancer, but that doesn't make it any less deadly.

Idol Makeover

One of our problems in identifying today's gods is that their identities not only lack the usual trappings of religion; they are also

---

*Hint: The answer isn't "a duck."

things that often aren't even wrong. Is God against pleasure? Sex? Money? Popularity?

These things are not immoral. They are morally neutral — and sometimes even commendable — until they become something else. It could be friendships or the pursuit of getting into your dream college. It could be a worthy cause. You could even be feeding the hungry and healing the sick. All of those are good things.

The problem is that the instant something takes the place of God, the moment it becomes an end in itself rather than something to lay at God's throne, it becomes an idol. When someone or something replaces the Lord God in the position of glory in our lives, then that person or thing by definition has become our god.

So to identify some gods, look at what you are chasing. Another way to identify the gods at war in your life is to look at what you create.

Remember your commandments. First: no other gods.

Second: no making other gods to worship.

The profound wisdom of that second commandment is that anything in the world can be hammered into an idol, and therefore can be a false god. It's DIY idolatry: choose from our handy assortment of gods, mix and match, create your own.

When God gave Moses the Ten Commandments on Mount Sinai, the people waiting below whined because it was taking so long. Moses had left his brother, Aaron, in charge, and the people began clamoring for a god to lead them. They gathered everyone's gold, put it on the fire, and made a golden calf to worship. A little bit ironic, don't you think? The very moment God was telling Moses about having no other gods before him, the people were down below rigging up a god.

Later in the Bible is a reflection on what these people did: "The people made a calf at Mount Sinai; they bowed before an image made of gold. They traded their glorious God for a statue of a grass-eating bull" (Psalm 106:19 – 20, NLT).

That's not a good trade. They traded the Creator God for a god of their own creation.

Are we really any different? We replace God with statues of our own creation.

The latest smartphone technology that keeps us from feeling left out.

Clothes that get us into the right clique.

Grades that push us higher up the class rankings.

A team that wins the championship.

A body that is toned and fit.

We work hard at molding and creating our golden calves.

I already hear what you're thinking: *"You could say that about anything. You could take any issue, anything someone devoted anything to, and make it out to be idolatry."*

Exactly.

Anything at all can become an idol once it becomes a substitute for God in our lives.

To describe the concept more clearly, anything that becomes the purpose or driving force of your life probably points back to idolatry of some kind. Think about what you have pursued and created, and ask yourself, *Why?*

If you have "hot button" issues that tend to get you upset, why?

If you plan to go shopping this weekend even though you have a closetful of clothes, why?

If you spend countless hours fixing up your car and redecorating your room, why?

To think of these things as forms of idolatry, we need to use new imagery. Discard the idea of golden cows and multi-armed figurines. Even, just for a moment, strip away the whole idea of idolatry as an item on a ten-point list of don'ts.

This next exercise may seem a bit weird, but stick with me. I want you to reimagine idolatry as a tree.

See it in your mind: one of those great oak trees that seem

older than time itself, one with impressive branches reaching out in every direction. And down below the surface, deep roots dig in and anchor it into place.

Imagine this tree of idolatry with many branches, each with something tied to it.

From one of the branches dangles a pot of gold.

Another branch grows entertainment all kinds. Xboxes (or, if you prefer, a PS4), tablets, computers, and every kind of technology imaginable seem to sprout from a different section of that branch.

Another branch widens into a flat, round ending, and when you move closer, you can see that it is really a mirror that shows an idealized reflection of yourself.

Yet another branch is carved with beautiful craftsmanship. You follow its sinuous lines and realize it is the image of two human figures, entwined in a sensuous embrace.

One branch has, as fruit, different sets of keys — one set to a sports car, another to your own apartment after graduation.

Quite a peculiar tree. It has many other branches, each one with a curious item attached to it.

Here's the point: Idolatry is the tree from which our sins and struggles grow. Idolatry is always the issue. It's the trunk of the tree, and all other problems are just branches.

the battleground
of the gods

How would you feel if your entire Internet search history was posted for the world to see?

That's what America Online* did. Remember this company? It's still around. But when the World Wide Web began to intertwine the earth, it was the first big search engine. Then a number of years ago, America Online released, to the public, the Internet search history of 650,000 of its network users. The company was trying to demonstrate its vast reach among consumers.

So if you typed "NFL football scores" into a browser window, it was now a matter of public record.

Already you're saying, "What were they thinking?" But the fact is, AOL had taken certain precautions. No real names were used — only user numbers. So it wasn't Bob down the street, but an anonymous "User #545354," who was checking to see if the Green Bay Packers won.

The problem was that the precautions weren't strong enough. *The New York Times* quickly demonstrated how it was possible to select a user number and put a name to it.

How could they do that? It was actually pretty simple. Let's say

---

*True story: At one point, AOL flooded mailboxes by sending numerous CDs to homes. Not sure who the marketing genius was behind this idea, but in the 1990s more than 50 percent of the CDs produced worldwide were AOL's free software CDs. We collected enough to play Frisbee golf with them when I was in high school.

User #545354 searched for "transmission problems 2002 Chevy Camaro." This wouldn't tell us much on its own, but AOL also revealed thousands of other searches by the same user.* Given enough information it wasn't too difficult to look at the searches and match them up to a specific person.

As you can guess, people didn't simply search for car information or sports scores. They also searched for silly things. Sad things. And many, many truly disturbing things.[3] Each user's "data trail" drew an unflinching picture of that person.

You could say we are defined by our searches.

What would your data trail say about you? Where does the search you are on lead?

What you are searching for and chasing after reveals which god is winning the war in your heart. If you think of your life as the battleground of the gods, your heart is Bunker Hill. It's where the gods gather and wage war. Whatever god wins the day claims the throne of your heart.

THE SEARCH CONTINUES

Google, Twitter, and several other Internet companies track the most searched keywords and topics from day to day, month to month, and year to year. Advertisers, political consultants, and culture watchers pay close attention to what the world is seeking.

At the end of 2011, *sex* and *video* each logged 338 million searches per month.

Porn: 277 million.

Products and celebrities such as the iPad or Lady Gaga often shoot to the top for short durations.

During a typical period, the singer Justin Bieber was the

---

* Likely searches that start with *M* for a Camaro driver: Metallica, mullet, muscle cars.

subject of more searches than God, at more than 30 million searches for Bieber to 20 million for God.*

---

* www.webupon.com

Since I can't check your search history, I want you to examine your heart to find out where your allegiance lies and where your glory goes. "Above all else, guard your heart, for everything you do flows from it" (Proverbs 4:23). Your heart defines and determines who you are, how you think, and what you do. Because everything flows from it, your heart is the frontline for the gods at war.

What do we mean when we speak of "the heart"? In science, we know that it's the blood-pumping organ that makes the body run. It doesn't think; it doesn't feel. But in Hebrew culture, the heart was seen differently. It was a metaphor for the center, or core, of a personality. It was the spiritual hub. The ancients knew that you could lightly touch the wrist and feel a soft beating — what we call a pulse. That same pulse could be felt in the neck and elsewhere. But place the hand over the heart, which is the center of a person, and that beating was more powerful. So it stood to reason that everything flowed from the heart — not only blood but personality, motives, emotions, and will. The Hebrews understood that all along. In Hebrew, the word *heart* means "the kernel of the nut." Your "heart" reflects your true identity.

Here's an example of the Hebrew idea: "As water reflects the face, so one's life reflects the heart" (Proverbs 27:19). The heart is the truth of your identity, that's why the gods fight so fiercely for every inch of it.

The Source

Let's think about your heart, and we'll do it by imagining a scenario. You're out for a hike on a beautiful spring day. You're delighted to hear running water, and sure enough, you come to a creek. But there's something wrong with this picture. You notice that someone has dumped trash into the stream. Judging by some of the empty soda cans, the trash has been there awhile.* And there is an ugly film on the top of the water.

You can't just leave the stream as you found it, because it would bother your conscience. So you stoop down and begin gathering the trash.

It takes several hours before you begin to see a difference — it's amazing how much junk is there. You sit back, rest for a moment, and realize you'll have to keep returning each day until the site is truly clean. Well, that's okay; it's a project you'll be proud of.

Except when you come back the next day, it's as if your work has been undone. In fact there's more trash than before. Somehow the garbage multiplied overnight. You think about the unlikelihood of someone coming to this very spot to dump garbage in the few hours while you were away.

Something smells fishy, you think. *And gross.*

So you begin to follow the creek upstream.

Sure enough, you come to a garbage dump that has been there for years. It's emptying into the passing creek, and your cleaning job only opened up a gap for more stuff to settle. You could go and clean every day, but it would just be like pushing a boulder up the hill and watching it roll back down again. Which can be surprisingly fun, but, really, what's the point?

If you want your creek to be clean, that means going directly to the source and dealing with what's there.

Think of your heart, as the Hebrews did, as the source from which your life flows — thoughts, emotions, actions.

How much of your life do you spend dealing with the visible

---

*Sprite Remix and Apple Slice (your parents *may* remember this failed soda), thanks for the memories. It's not the same without you.

garbage rather than what produces it? We often spend great amounts of time, money, energy, and frustration doing trash removal when something upstream is still dumping into the flow. A lot of times your parents, and even the church, tend to focus downstream too much. It's so much easier to pick up a little bit of trash. Dealing with what's upstream is a staggering commitment. But the gods know the heart is the battlefield. It's where the war is won.

Overlooking the heart and focusing just on what's downstream could be described as "behavior modification." Behavior modification, popular in mid-twentieth century psychology, is the idea of trying to bring about change by targeting things we can observe and measure. It's symptom-based care, quick-fix methodology.

Here are some examples of how we do trash removal:

- If you do poorly on tests, you commit to studying harder the night before.
- If you have an anger problem, you take a deep breath and count to ten.
- If profanities pour profusely from your mouth, you start a "cuss jar" and throw in a dollar every time you trip up.
- If you're hung up with how you look, you go to school without makeup.
- If you're addicted to video games, you set a timer and only play an hour a day.

This is not a condemnation of setting limits or working harder or "cuss jars." All of these things can be positive, just as cleaning up the downstream trash is something that must be done. It's simply that the heart of the issue is an issue of the heart.

Walk Upstream

Take a few minutes and consider your life. Get past trash removal for a moment and hike upstream to the heart of the problem.

Perhaps there has been a lot of drama in your life lately. If you and I were to talk, you might say, "I love the Lord. I don't have any issues with idolatry. My problem is that I just tend to worry too much. I become very anxious."

Okay, but hike upstream. What is it in your heart that is causing all that worry? It could be that if you stopped and examined your heart deeply enough, you would find a deep need to be in control of things. You like every *i* to be dotted, every *t* to be crossed. A place for everything and everything in its place.* You don't like surprises, and you simply want life to go according to script.

No law against any of that, right? As a matter of fact, teachers love people like you. They describe you as highly responsible — someone good with details. But still, you don't enjoy the restless nights, the way the wheels just keep turning in your mind, the fact that you feel no real peace.

The need for control is a relentless god that has taken ground in your heart. In fact the more control you crave, the more that craving will control you, thus making "control" your god.

Because gods at times form dark alliances of cooperation with each other, maybe the god of control is working with the god of comfort, because your need to cover every detail speaks of a drive to stay snug within your comfort zone. And so you think the issue is anxiety, while perhaps the real issue is that the gods of control and comfort are winning the war for your heart.

And these gods want to take your life in a much different direction than the Lord God. God is often calling us outside our comfort zones. He's calling us to a great adventure that requires

---

* Unnecessary and pointless footnotes are irritating. Couldn't agree more.

risk and faith. Jesus' invitation is to take up a cross and follow him — but it's hard to carry a cross when comfort is your god. The gods of control and comfort are likely in direct conflict with the Lord God who has called you to a new kind of life.

Let's try another example. What if you come to me and tell me that you are an overachiever? "That's my problem, plain and simple," you say. "I have to be the best. How can I stop being so driven to perfection?"

My first impulse is to do some trash removal, so I tell you to pursue the discipline of cutting down your extracurriculars. You will still be able to get into a good college *without* being president of math club, student body president, golf team captain, a mentor to blind students, and an AP scholar with distinction. Plus, getting a B on a test shouldn't send you into a depression and cause you to lose sleep, thinking of what you could've done differently and worrying how much your grade point will move. Symptom stuff.

But journey upstream and you'll likely find that being an overachiever isn't really the problem, "plain and simple." There are probably some false gods backstage in your life, creating havoc. What motivations would make someone an overachiever? It could be pride and the need to be number one no matter the cost. That's definitely an idol.

Or it could be that grades and class rank aren't really what overachievement is all about for you. You could actually be serving the god of perfectionism. Are you one of those people who is never happy with the results, who thinks it should be done better?

What about the god of power? Maybe you're getting caught up in accumulating as much control as possible because power is important.

Behind all of these, of course, could be that incredibly pervasive god of "me." Are you building a monument to your own abilities and personal value through how well you do your schoolwork and perform in your other activities?

It all comes down to what's happening in your heart. And that's why Jesus put so much emphasis there. He wasn't quick to reward good behavior if the heart wasn't right. In Matthew 15:8 Jesus said of the religious leaders, "These people honor me with their lips, but their hearts are far from me." Later in the chapter Jesus says, "Don't you see that whatever enters the mouth goes into the stomach and then out of the body? But the things that come out of a person's mouth come from the heart, and these defile them. For out of the heart come evil thoughts — murder, adultery, sexual immorality, theft, false testimony, slander" (Matthew 15:17 – 19).

We want to focus on the outside, but Jesus makes the point that it's all about what's inside. The heart is the battleground for the gods because everything flows from it.

I was talking to a friend who is a cardiologist. He was telling me about a procedure called an arteriogram that is used to diagnose the health of a heart. Here's how it works: He injects a dye into the bloodstream, then an X-ray is taken of the arteries to locate any blockages. Once they locate a blockage, he inserts a stent through the patient's leg and opens up the blood vessel.

But frequently a heart problem goes undetected and undiagnosed for years. No arteriogram is done to test the heart. Why? Because the symptoms don't seem relevant. A patient may face insomnia, back pain, a loss of appetite, anxiety, vision problems, and other challenges. The patient seeks medical help to treat the symptoms. They think they have a sleeping issue or a back pain issue or a vision issue, when in truth it's a heart issue. It's cardiovascular, and until that is addressed, the patient isn't going to get better.

A Spiritual Arteriogram

It's difficult to see ourselves as idol worshipers. Whatever our symptoms might be, we struggle to connect them to the throne of the heart and what occupies it. But that is where the battle is being fought. So I want to ask you to do a spiritual arteriogram to discover your heart health. I'm going to ask you a series of questions that only you can answer.

Think of these questions as dye being injected into your bloodstream to help reveal and locate some problem areas.

What Disappoints You?

When we feel overwhelmed by disappointment, it's a good sign that something has become far more important to us than it should be. Disproportionate disappointment reveals that we have placed intense hope and longing in something other than God.

So if you were to identify your greatest disappointments, where would you point? The realm of friendship? Erwin Lutzer writes, "Have you ever thought that our disappointments are God's way of reminding us that there are idols in our lives that must be dealt with?"[4]

What Do You Complain About the Most?

This question is similar to the last, but we're looking at the outside this time — what you express. This might be a good time to get an objective opinion. Ask someone close to you, who you trust to be honest, about your typical complaints.

If you constantly complain about your lack of money, or not having the newest version of something, maybe materialism has become too important to you.

If you constantly complain about not getting enough respect from friends or feeling like you're left out, maybe what other people think about you matters more than it should.

If you constantly complain about not getting enough playing time or not making first string, maybe sports has become your god.

What we complain about reveals what really matters to us. Whining shows what has power over us.

Whining, in many ways, is the opposite of worshiping the Lord. Worship is when we glorify God for who he is and acknowledge what he has done for us, but whining is ignoring who God is and forgetting what he has done for us.

Where Do You Spend Your Money?

More on this later, but it's important enough to touch on now because the Bible says where your treasure is, that's where your heart is also. Where your money goes shows what god is winning your heart. So take a look at your closet, on your computer, or in your driveway. Examine your spending habits (or what you have your parents spend on your behalf, if that's the case) to find out what is most important to you.

What Worries You?

It could be the idea of losing someone significant, losing your place on the team, or losing your scholarship or your talent. It could be the fear of being ridiculed. Maybe it's the fear of being alone. You can care so deeply about something that it has a hold on you deep inside and is revealed when your mind is in free-form mode at night. Whatever it is that wakes you — or for that matter keeps you up — has the potential to be an idol.

Where Is Your Sanctuary?

Where do you go when you're hurting?

Let's say it's been a terrible day at school. You come home and go — where? To the refrigerator for comfort food like ice cream? To the phone to vent with your most trusted friend? Do you seek escape in novels or movies or video games or drugs? Where do you look for emotional rescue?

The Bible tells us that God is our refuge and strength, our help in times of trouble — so much so that we will not fear though the mountains fall into the heart of the sea (Psalm 46:1 – 2). That strikes me as a good place to run. But it's so easy to forget, so natural for us to run in other directions. Where we go says a lot about who we are. The "high ground" we seek reveals the geography of our values.

When I was interviewed for my current job, the elders of the church asked me various questions. One seemed particularly important to them: Tell us about your sufferings and hardships.

I thought about it and came up with a challenge or two I'd faced, but had to admit I'd never really suffered. One of the elders was concerned about that response. I thought, *What am I supposed to do? Go lose a loved one?*

Since he kept pushing the issue, he finally explained, "You don't know who people really are until they've suffered."

A few weeks later, I came home from work and went upstairs to wake up Morgan from her nap. She was two at the time. I saw that her five-foot-tall pine dresser had fallen over, and then I realized she was under it. My heart almost stopped. I frantically moved the furniture and saw that my daughter was black and blue.

We rushed her to the hospital and did a flurry of tests and X-rays. Nothing was broken. She was breathing but unresponsive. Nerve damage was likely. I remember sitting in that dark hospital hall as they took her in for the initial X-rays. I was on the floor with my back against the wall, crying and praying. I began to sing, "Our God Is an Awesome God."

A week later, though my daughter was awake, she was unable to walk. Her left leg just wouldn't move. I kept praying, clinging to God. As time went on, she improved. She's fine these days, but I realized along the way that the elder had been right. I needed to learn something about myself, see how things would be between God and me when life got hard.

I discovered he would be my sanctuary even if my deepest fears were realized.

What Infuriates You?

Everyone has a hot button or two — something that we say "makes us crazy." Are you so competitive that you can't stand for your team to lose a game during gym class? Could it be that being the best is your idol? How do you respond to waiting in line to buy a shirt at the mall? When someone cuts in front of you, or decides to pay for everything in loose change, do you lose control over your emotions? What about when someone embarrasses you or doesn't treat you with respect? What's the real issue here? Maybe your quick temper reveals the oldest idol of them all — the god of me.

What Are Your Dreams?

If nightmares are revealing, so are daydreams — the places we choose for our imagination to go. What fantasy has a grip on you and puts a twinkle in your eye? Do you dream of being the next American Idol, or maybe a first-round draft pick? Aspirations are fine, but the question to ask is why you aspire to those things. Is your motivation to give God glory or is your motivation your own glory, fame, and fortune?

a jealous god

Michael Jordan may be the best basketball player of all time. With six NBA championships, five Most Valuable Player awards, fourteen All-Star Game appearances, and more than 32,000 points scored, it's hard to argue that he wasn't at least one of the greatest. An entire generation of kids grew up wanting to be "like Mike."*

In his book *Driven from Within*, Jordan tells an eye-opening story about a visit he made to a friend's home. Fred Whitfield was the president and chief operating officer of another NBA team. The two of them were getting ready to go out to dinner when Jordan said, "Man, it's kind of cold. Can I borrow one of your jackets?"

Whitfield said, "Sure," and told him where the coat closet was. Jordan disappeared down the hall, and the house fell silent for a moment. Then the star reappeared, carrying an armful of branded athletic jackets, shirts, shoes, and other gear. He dumped the whole pile on the floor and disappeared down the hall again for more.

Whitfield looked at the heap and noted that all the items were made by Puma. Jordan was linked mind, body, and soul to Nike. When he'd found that the closet had materials made by both manufacturers, he did not approve. The Nike items were there because Whitfield was a close friend of Michael Jordan. The Puma stuff had come as the result of his close friendship with Ralph Sampson, an ex-player who promoted that brand.

---

*Why do I suddenly want some Gatorade?

Whitfield stood and waited to see what Jordan would do. The star walked into the kitchen, came out with a butcher knife, and cut the pile of gear on the floor into thousands of pieces.

When he had thoroughly destroyed the athletic gear, he gathered it all up again and carried it to a trash can for disposal.

When he was done, Jordan returned to Whitfield's side and said, "Hey, dude, call [my Nike representative] tomorrow and tell him to replace all of this. But don't ever let me see you again in anything other than Nike. You can't ride the fence."[5]

Jordan's behavior is a little uncomfortable to read about, isn't it? I find that people who follow Christ, people who read books like this one, are polite people. I can't imagine myself pulling a Michael Jordan in someone's house, nor would I recommend it to those who wish to keep their friends.

But don't you think Jordan offers us a pretty good picture of idol smashing? He demonstrates total commitment. And really that's the kind of radical commitment God longs for from his people. He doesn't want us to just make room in our closet for him; he wants the closet to himself.

Already you can probably see a problem. *Committed* isn't a word that's often used to describe people nowadays. Though perhaps you have grandparents, or perhaps great-grandparents, who were part of what's called the "Greatest Generation" — the one that fought the Second World War. This group of people was known for commitment. They worked one job, lived in one home, and attended one church for the duration of their adulthood. People were committed to companies, communities, congregations, and their families.

In our times, families commonly live a nomadic existence, moving from city to city and from church to church. Our eyes are always on the horizon, looking for the better cell phone, the cuter boyfriend or girlfriend, the happier life. We're always watching for a better deal. We live in a world where "no strings attached" is a popular choice when it comes to relationships. We seem to be a generation with one commitment: keeping our options open.

While keeping our options open is not necessarily all bad, we should recognize that this quality makes it much more difficult to appreciate the seriousness of idolatry. The only relationship God is interested in is one that is exclusive and completely committed. He is not interested in an "open relationship" with you. He won't consider sharing space on the loveseat of your heart.

His throne has only one seat.

Hey Jealousy ...

You shall not make for yourself an [idol] in the form of anything. . . . You shall not bow down to them or worship them; for I, the LORD your God, am a jealous God.
— Exodus 20:4–5

Wouldn't it be interesting if people were not only called by their given names but also by their most dominant personality traits? If that was the case, what would your best friend's name be? Maybe something complimentary like *good listener, always loyal,* or *kindhearted.* Or maybe it would be something a little less complimentary.*

In Scripture, the Lord God is often named by his character qualities. He is the "King of Kings," "Deliverer," "Provider," "Healer," and "Redeemer." The list goes on and on. Yet of all the names of God, there is one that seems out of place. Exodus 34:14 reads, "Do not worship any other god, for the Lord, whose name is Jealous, is a jealous God."

Jealous? That word doesn't seem very ... well, positive. It feels petty — like a couple of junior high girls who are both interested in the same boy; like a basketball player who avoids passing the ball

---

* *Back-stabber, time waster, self-absorbed*

to the teammate who keeps getting the high score; like a possessive high school boyfriend who becomes upset if his girlfriend makes eye contact with another guy.

Besides, what reason would God have to be jealous? Doesn't everything already belong to him? Is there anything that competes with his power or his greatness? Of course not — at least not in reality.

But what about in your heart?

God is jealous for your heart, not because he is petty or insecure, but because he loves you. The reason why God has such a huge problem with idolatry is that his love for you is all-consuming. He loves you too much to share you.

Paul Copan, a philosophy professor at Palm Beach Atlantic University, asks the question, *When can jealousy be a good thing?*

He describes God's deep passion for our wholehearted devotion. People, he says, are like the dog who drinks out of the toilet bowl and says, "It doesn't get much better than this!" We could be enjoying the living water that only Christ can offer, yet we choose substitutes that are shockingly, disgustingly inferior.[6] God knows what he has in mind for us, and it grieves him to see the choices we make in ignorance. It makes him jealous, in the most righteous and loving way.

IT'S NOT EASY BEING GREEN

God can do jealousy, we cannot. The green-eyed monster can easily consume us when we're jealous of our friends' possessions or popularity. Jealousy is such a strong emotion that it can affect us physically and emotionally.

- Neuroscientist Hidehiko Takahashi of Kyoto University says the neural nodes in our brains associated with fear, anger, and disgust start firing like crazy when jealousy is

---

introduced. Social pain is experienced in much the same way as physical pain.

- Our stomachs tighten up when we're jealous, resulting in cramping and a loss of appetite.
- Our nervous system can also buckle under the stress of jealousy. Jonathan Dvash, a neuroscientist at the University of Haifa, says jealousy can cause the heart to race and blood pressure to spike.

Katherine Schreiber, "Carnal Clues: Seeing Green," *Psychology Today*, March 12, 2012.

And here's what is said of God: "For the Lord your God is a consuming fire, a jealous God" (Deuteronomy 4:24).

In the Bible, the words *jealous* and *zealous* are basically interchangeable — it's the same Hebrew word in the original texts. In English, we spell the two almost the same because they derive from the same Greek root. We think of zeal as intense enthusiasm. That idea captures why God is so possessive about us: He is, as he says, a consuming fire of passion for us.

Have you ever seen someone who's fallen deeply in love* — who is so consumed by those feelings that it's all he or she ever talks about? Well, that's only the barest shadow of God's love for you. We need to remember, as we talk about God's intolerance of idolatry, that everything comes back to a passionate love that is so immense, so powerful, that it burns hotter than a billion suns.

I hope you'll think about that as you read this book, because here is what will happen. As we walk through the temples of the modern gods in these pages, you'll recognize the ones that are at war in your life. And God will speak. He'll challenge you with two words: you choose.

---

* We're talking about more than an undying crush here — though those people can be pretty intense in their feelings too. (Mention Ryan Gosling to some people at your own peril.)

You choose between me and working an after-school job just so you have money to spend on the things you want.

You choose between me and your athletic aspirations.

You choose between me and that relationship.

If you keep watch over your own heart, you'll face those fork-in-the-road moments. He won't give you the option of making him one of many gods. There is no room for anyone or anything but himself. That's how much he loves you.

Idolatry Is Adultery

The prophet Ezekiel used a powerful analogy to describe what idolatry feels like to God. He compared it to a cheating spouse. This analogy runs all through the Scriptures. In the New Testament, the church is described as the bride of Christ, and many of Jesus' parables revolve around a bride being faithful as she awaits her bridegroom.

The pain of having an unfaithful partner is one of the most agonizing human experiences. It's the ultimate betrayal. Yet this is how we are described when we reject the love of God for cheap substitutes. God is the betrayed lover.

As I discussed this concept with our church, I asked everybody to imagine going to a local restaurant and seeing me having a romantic candlelight dinner with a woman who is not my wife. Then, I said, imagine walking up and asking me, "Who are you with and what's this all about?"

Picture me smiling nonchalantly and saying, "Oh, I'm on a date."

"But what about your wife?"

"What about her? I love her too. I've taken her out plenty of times."

I'm pretty sure you'd walk away angry and disgusted, and you'd have good reason.

Can you imagine my wife, afterward, meeting me at the door

with a big smile? She would say, "Hi, honey. Did you have a good time on your date?"*

Her hurt, her anger, and her pain would be enormous. And in fact I would be offended if she didn't feel that way. If she was anything other than jealous, it would show me that she didn't really care.

It's overwhelming to realize that the Lord God loves us this way. It changes the way we see ourselves. Everything in life has more significance when someone loves you like that — especially God himself.

And he does, of course. He isn't happy to be one of many gods that we worship. He makes it clear that we are to love him with all our heart, soul, mind, and strength. That statement is often given as the positive summary of the Ten Commandments. The negatively stated summary would be this: "You will have no other gods before me." There is no cohabitation. There is no open marriage.

Hot Pursuit

The jealousy of God is demonstrated not just in the offense he takes at our idolatry, but in his pursuit of our hearts. He doesn't just let you run off with someone else; he relentlessly chases after you. No matter what god seems to be winning the war for your heart at this moment, you can be sure of one thing — the one true God will not give up without a fight. God is in pursuit of our wandering, cheating hearts, and he will stalk us to our graves.

You can't understand the seriousness of idolatry without understanding the jealousy of God. And you can't understand his jealousy without some understanding of his relentless, powerful love for you. The two are intertwined.

The entire Bible is a love letter to humanity in the form of a

---

*News flash: this would never, ever happen.

story, so we'll see what God has seen since he first created us, and so we'll know all the ways we've insulted his love and all the ways he has redoubled his pursuit. This is a God who gives us the freedom to say no but insists on giving us every possible, conceivable chance to say yes.

The Old Testament is a story of our foolish, self-destructive rebellion as God's people. He offers us a special relationship, and time after time we take his gifts and turn away, choosing one idol or another instead of the amazing opportunity he has for us. By the end of the Old Testament, people have turned so far away from God that heaven seems silent. There are no more prophets. There is no more deliverance from enemies. God seems to have abandoned the human race, though in truth it's just the opposite.

And then God, in the deepest and most startling expression of his relentless pursuit, sends his own Son. God is back, and this time, it's personal.* Of course, it's always been that way for him. But now God has put everything on the line. He has given his one and only Son. Being God, and knowing all things, he knew exactly how it would turn out. He knew about the arrest, the unfair trial, the beatings, the mocking, the crucifixion.

The event of the coming of Jesus represents just how far God is willing to go to win your heart. He had to make a choice, a choice between your heart and the life of his Son. "God so loved the world that he gave his one and only Son" (John 3:16).

Can you feel him coming after you? Can you hear his footfalls? Can you feel the whisper that says, "I will not take no for an answer"?

In Charles Dickens's novel *David Copperfield*, a family lives by the sea in an old, abandoned boat.† Maybe you've had to read this classic literary work in school. In it, the father figure, who is an

---

*Imagine the deep voice of a movie trailer announcer saying this.
†Then a famous magician comes by and makes the boat disappear. Just kidding.

aging fisherman, has adopted his nephew and niece. The niece is named Emily, and he dotes on her. His greatest aspiration is to see her married and happy with a fine young man.

But Emily has other ideas. She is taken in by a fast-talking, handsome man who promises to marry her and show her the great sights of the world, if she'll run away with him. She does, but it soon becomes clear that he has no intention of marrying her. And, since this is the mid-1800s, her name is ruined, and the name of her humble family is ruined. She has messed up so badly that she doesn't even think about going home. Often in those days, a young lady had no recourse but prostitution. And that's what happens to Emily.

Her grief-stricken uncle understands all this, but it makes no difference. He takes every penny to his name and leaves to search the entire world for his niece. If that takes the rest of his life, so be it. He will visit every dark, seedy street corner in every town in Europe until he finds her, because his love for her is completely unaffected by what she has done. He simply can't stand to lose her. He searches for many years, until all his hairs are gray. Finally he locates her and brings her home. She can't believe he had come searching for her or that anyone would care about her. But he is happier than he has ever been, because his child has come home.

Jesus told a similar story about a prodigal son who left and blew his inheritance on wild parties and fast living. But when he returned, his father ran out to meet him. That's our God — our jealous, insistent, loving God. While we were yet sinners, Christ died for us. While we were yet sinners, God kept coming. And he still does. He is doing so in my life and in yours. He hates everything that becomes an obstacle between you and him, everything that blocks your view of him or threatens to keep you from hearing his voice. He wants you, and not just some of you.

He is jealous for your whole heart.

calling all gods

Kylie Bisutti knew exactly what goals she was pursuing. She wanted to be a fashion model, and she succeeded at the highest level. In 2009, at age nineteen, Bisutti won a competition against ten thousand rivals in the Victoria's Secret Model Search. Victoria's Secret, of course, is an American lingerie retailer that makes over five billion dollars a year. It's known for its racy fashion shows, its catalogues, and of course its "angels" — models who often become fashion icons.*

"Victoria's Secret was my absolute biggest goal in life," she said. "It was all I ever wanted career-wise. I actually loved it while I was there."

Just before her modeling dreams came true, Bisutti got married. She and her husband were followers of Christ, and she couldn't help but think about what she was doing. What kind of example was she setting? She realized there was a great deal of difference between modeling clothing and flaunting provocative undergarments.

She came to the conclusion that her body was for her husband to see, and not for millions of strangers on the Internet. She also realized she cared deeply about the legions of young Christian girls who looked up to her. She worried that it could cause them to begin choosing skimpy, suggestive clothing because of her example.

---

* So I've been told.

There was something else too. "I finally achieved my biggest dream," she said, "the dream that I always wanted. But when I finally got it, it wasn't all that I thought it would be."

Stop. Go back. Read that sentence again. You're not gonna do it, are you? Then let me give it to you again: "I finally achieved my biggest dream," she said, "the dream that I always wanted. But when I finally got it, it wasn't all that I thought it would be." How many times have we heard that? Someone has a dream. They yearn for it. They reach for it. They give all they have to attain it. And it doesn't measure up.

Her greatest goal was unmasked as just another god that couldn't deliver.

Kylie's dreams had come true, only for her to reach the conclusion that they were the wrong dreams, even if millions of other women shared them. She knew that following Jesus and giving glory to the Lord God meant turning away from the gods that so many people spend their lives bowing down to. Ultimately it became a worship choice. So she turned in her wings and stepped down from lingerie modeling.[7]

Have you ever had a moment like the one Kylie had, when you realized you had to make a choice and your entire future hinged on the choice you made? That if you went to a certain university, joined a certain traveling sports team, made a certain ethical decision, pursued a certain person to date, then the ramifications for your future would be immense?

Sometimes we stand at those forks in the road and know exactly what's at stake. But so many other times, we just keep walking, wandering down a particular path without really thinking about it. We make many choices without even being aware that we are choosing. We do things because that's the way our family has always done them. Or because that's the way other people, people we admire, do them. Or because these days almost everyone does them that way.

Whether or not we are aware of it, it turns out that, just like Kylie, we regularly make choices that declare which gods are winning the war in our lives.

Doors 1, 2, and 3

Moses led the homeless nation of Israel out of Egypt, where the people had been enslaved for generations. God demonstrated his power through the ten plagues, the splitting of the Red Sea, the provision of food from heaven, and the pouring of water from a rock. He even provided them with a supernatural GPS system by leading them with a cloud during the day and a pillar of fire at night.

But the people still didn't have much faith. They constantly whined and complained. It should have been about a month-long hike to the Promised Land, but God caused them to wander in the wilderness for nearly forty years. This was basically a camping trip that lasted four decades. Moses and his generation died before entering the land God had promised Abraham hundreds of years earlier. Joshua replaced Moses as the leader of God's people and brought them into the Promised Land.

By the time we come to Joshua 24, Joshua is pushing 110 years old. He has led a life of great faith. For example, when twelve spies were dispatched into Canaan to scout the land, ten came back and said, "No way can we pull this off. Those are giants in there." Joshua and a guy named Caleb discounted any opposition, as long as God was with them. They trusted the Lord and feared nothing.

By this time in his life, Joshua has been a general through many wars. He fought off hostile tribes who sought to destroy the Israelites. He saw the walls of Jericho come thundering down in miraculous fashion. He fought battles and bears the scars, as well as the wisdom and faith that grows and deepens with struggle.

Joshua seems to know he doesn't have much time left in this world. He gathers the people of Israel together, clears his throat, and speaks with power: "Now fear the Lord and serve him with all faithfulness. Throw away the gods your ancestors worshiped beyond the Euphrates River and in Egypt, and serve the Lord. But if serving the Lord seems undesirable to you, then choose for yourselves this day whom you will serve, whether the gods your ancestors served beyond the Euphrates, or the gods of the Amorites, in whose land you are living. But as for me and my household, we will serve the Lord" (Joshua 24:14 – 15).

Joshua doesn't tiptoe around what he wants to say. He gets right to the point and throws down a challenge: It's time for the people to make a choice. The people can follow the Lord God, the God of Abraham, Isaac, and Jacob, or they can choose a different god. It's time to accept a worldview and allow it to remake them.

"It's up to you," Joshua is saying. "But I can tell you this much. As for me and my house, our decision is made. We know whom we will serve — but you must make your own choice."

I find it interesting that Joshua gives three options along with the one true God. When I offer an invitation to salvation in church, I don't make it multiple choice. But even though Joshua is a commander who's used to giving orders, he knows that a personal choice must be made. No one can be ordered into the kingdom of God. No one can be driven there or carried bodily over the threshold. It's a path that individuals must choose, at the expense of all other paths.

So Joshua lays it out. He shows the people what's behind the other three doors by breaking it down this way:

- Follow the old gods from beyond the river, from the place where you started out.
- Follow the gods you met next, in Egypt, where you were enslaved.
- Follow the local gods, those of the people recently defeated by the one true God.

At first glance, we read that and think, *No problem for me. I don't worship Egyptian or "local" gods, or any from "beyond the river."* But forget the details for a moment, and notice that each category has to do with a time and a place of life. This is highly significant.

The gods that compete for our attention come at us based on the circumstances of our everyday existence. They may have made a few costume changes over the years, but the categories are the same.

No Choice but to Choose

We will consider what's behind each of the doors Joshua mentions, but first, it's important to understand the easily missed underlying assumption — and it's something I've already assumed in this book: You *will* make a choice.

Joshua doesn't go through the list and say, "Or you could just choose not to worship anything at all." All of us are worshipers. Worship is hardwired into who we are. It's true of every culture and every civilization — everyone worships. When I was in college, I spent a month in Africa with a medical missions team. We went off-road and visited several tribes that had no contact with the outside world. As we entered their communities, the question was not, "Are they worshipers?" The question was, "Who or what do they worship?"

Wherever you go, you see that people have chosen. You will too. You can go to places where they have old-school idols, rituals, and sacrifices. Or you can go to the most technologically advanced cities, where folks think they're way past that "religious mumbo jumbo" — though they would probably say something more intelligent sounding than "mumbo jumbo."* But upon closer inspection you will find that they are sacrificing a great deal on the altars of power or pleasure or finance. It's really all the same. People are

---

*They would probably say gobbledygook, hooey, hogwash, or poppycock.

choosing their gods and bringing their offerings. At the end of the day, the real offering is themselves.

Peter Kreeft, a philosopher, puts it this way: "The opposite of theism is not atheism, it's idolatry." In other words, everyone is going to worship a god. We were created to be worshipers, as birds were created to fly and rivers were created to flow. It's what we do. The question for you is who or what will be the object of your worship.

Stop and pay attention to the advertising on TV. All of the products are being marketed to the worshiper in us. Companies make their products sound suspiciously like saviors. The not-so-subtle message of nearly every advertisement is: If you're unhappy, bored, or depressed, then buy this product. You will be saved from your unhappiness, boredom, and depression. This product is here to redeem you, to deliver you. Drink this beer to be cool. Wear these clothes to be popular. Eat at this restaurant to be happy. Drive this car to be powerful.

They even offer an invitation: Dial this number. Visit this dealer. Order online today. Don't wait — call now. You half expect them to end the commercial by saying, "Can I get an amen?"

Life presents us infinite choices. There are lots of options, with one exception: the option to opt out. Again, there is no box for "none of the above." Joshua says, "Pick one." If we set this scene in a modern context, we would expect a little pushback on this question. Someone would raise his hand and say, "That's all cool and everything, Josh, but we're not really into worship. See, we're just not really the religious types."

And there would be lots of nodding heads and "what-he-saids" from the rest of the crowd. "Religion is cool for you and your house, but me and my house just aren't into that."

Here's where we get confused; in our modern thinking, we associate worship with religion. But since we all worship, everybody follows a religion. It may be the religion of pleasure, or money, or relationships. So Joshua truly is speaking to all of us when he says, "Choose for yourselves this day whom you will serve." Otherwise you will float through life, until you find yourself inside a temple bowing to a god you never consciously chose.

Four Points on a Compass

Joshua calls the people to choose, and he points to four options. Think of these options as four points on a compass: whatever you choose is going to lead you in a different direction than the others. A lot is at stake because the choice you make will ultimately determine where you end up.

OPTION 1: Gods of Our Fathers (and Mothers)

"The gods your ancestors worshiped beyond the Euphrates River."
— Joshua 24:14

Long before God spoke to Abraham about the future of his people — a people with a special standing before God — the ancestors of Abraham worshiped the gods of their land. In the Mesopotamian area, there was a god for nearly every conceivable purpose. There were three "cosmic" deities, three "astral" ones, and a whole slew of specialized gods and corresponding demons. Dead people came back as spirits to haunt their children. Hills and rocks and mountains were considered to be alive and to have powers.[8]

Abraham came from a society that believed in those gods. In fact the Bible specifically tells us that Abraham's father was an idol worshiper. Belief in these gods persisted even after the rise of the Hebrew people, through the time of Egyptian slavery, and up to Joshua's era. Now, Joshua wants to know if the people are simply going to default to the gods of their forefathers.

It's still a valid question, isn't it? Our parents raise us in their faith — or the lack thereof. We may not do so consciously, but we constantly erect idols in our lives and follow what we were told is worthy of our worship.

Think about how this is true in the family you live in. Is it possible that the gods that are at war in your life today are the same gods your parents or grandparents worshiped when you were younger?

I recently saw a title on the cover of a magazine that read, "My DNA Made Me Do It." The article basically said you can thank your parents for all your problems. But one big thing they touched on was that your mother and your father contributed some twenty-three thousand chromosomes to you. Some of what you inherited from them is easy to see. You've got your dad's nose or your mom's hair. But that's not all you picked up from them. We often end up worshiping whatever god they worshiped.

Psychology would affirm the likelihood of this transference. It's called the "law of exposure." The basic premise is that our lives are determined by our thoughts, and our thoughts are determined by what we are exposed to. The law of exposure means that our minds absorb and our lives ultimately reflect whatever we most frequently experience. It shouldn't be surprising then that we have a tendency to worship the gods of our fathers and mothers.

Perhaps nothing is more important to your dad than a successful career. His life revolves around his job. He is willing to sacrifice days off and family vacations to work his way up the corporate ladder. His mood is determined by what kind of day he had at work. His temple is his office, and he worships there sixty hours a week. And now, is it possible that you worship the god of success? Instead of finding your identity and worth in Christ, do you find it in your achievements?

Maybe your mom cares, or even obsesses, about appearances. Everything has to be perfect before company comes over, and she always updates the house. No one goes out in public without every hair perfectly in place. If a neighbor up the street buys a new SUV, your mom soon wants the same model with all the upgrades. She spends a lot of time and money to make sure all of you wear the right clothes from the right stores. Is it possible that you worship the gods of appearance and perfection? Instead of finding your identity and worth in Christ, do you find it in the clothes you wear, the house you live in, and what other people think of you?

Does your dad worship sports? Sex? Money? Status? Beer?

Does your mom worship shopping? Career? Children? Entertainment?

Don't just skip over these examples. Think about what is held up for you in your home. The most natural path in the world is to adopt the gods of our parents.

OPTION 2: Gods of Your Past

"The gods your ancestors worshiped ... in Egypt."
— Joshua 24:14

Joshua specifically mentions the gods from Egypt. These were the gods of the previous generation, gods from the past that never went away.

Like the Mesopotamians, the Egyptians had a diverse and highly developed pantheon of deities. For some reason, they loved mixing and matching human and animal body parts. Horus, god of the delta, had a human body with a falcon head.* Hathor, his partner, had the body of a cow and the head of a woman.†[9] You might call these the Transformers of the ancient world. The Egyptians had their popular gods, but they actually worshiped nearly everything, including the sun, moon, and stars.

The Hebrews lived in Egypt longer than the United States has been a nation. There was no way they were going to endure that period without absorbing some of the culture around them. Even when Moses led his people out of that land, the gods weren't

---

* Admittedly, that is awesome looking.
† Which is why you don't know any women named Hathor.

about to give up without a fight. Old habits, including old worship patterns, die hard. In Ezekiel 20:7, God says "Each of you, get rid of the vile images you have set your eyes on, and do not defile yourselves with the idols of Egypt. I am the Lord your God." Do you ever find yourself struggling with things from the past that you thought you had left behind a long time ago? When I was in high school, I remember being on my way to pick up a girl for a date. Naturally, I had to walk through her front yard. It was a minefield of doggie-doo. Being nervous about the date, of course, I wasn't watching where my big feet took me.

Her mom answered the door, smiled politely, and invited me in. As I sat on the sofa next to my date, I noticed a certain unpleasant aroma. I had no clue about its source. I sniffed my date, which, in retrospect, wasn't a good move. I leaned toward her parents — no, they were in the clear. The source of the smell was me. — I was ground zero! I looked down at my Doc Martins and realized that I had really stepped in it this time. Quite literally. In horror, I looked behind me and realized I had tracked animal excrement through the entryway, across the carpet, and into the living room. Suddenly I wasn't breathing well.

Here's my point: A lot of people become Christians. They invite Jesus Christ to come into their lives, to take the throne of their heart. Everything is great, but then they catch a strange whiff of something and realize they've brought stuff with them. Stuff that is embarrassing. Stuff that is fragrant, and not in a good way. Stuff that should have been destroyed a long time ago but managed to come along for the ride.

It's hard to understand, because they know their sins are forgiven. If they've been thoroughly cleaned, why is this stuff still clinging to them? In many ways, they haven't changed since conversion; they still have the old desires and habits. They've invited one Lord into their lives, but they're still paying attention to the old gods. That is the challenge for many of us: The problem isn't that we need to choose to follow Jesus; the problem is that we have tried to follow him without leaving something behind.

In Joshua's speech, he knows that there's a bit of Egypt still clinging to the sandals of his people. Old gods die hard. They hold on, they creep in, they quietly clutch at us. Perhaps when we meet Christ, the old gods fall silent for a while. But they regroup. They wait for their time, and they aim as high as ever. They want to rule our hearts again.

So even if you've chosen the Lord God in the past, the challenge of Joshua is to choose *this day* whom you will serve.

OPTION 3: Gods of Our Culture

"Or the gods of the Amorites, in whose land you are living."
— Joshua 24:15

Behind the third door were the newcomers to this cosmic clash. These were the gods of the land the Israelites had just fought so hard to conquer. Whereas the Egyptians once had the upper hand on God's people, these new gods were of the people the Israelites had defeated. They were pushed back, overcome, and yet they would continue to be a thorn in Israel's side for the rest of Old Testament times. Their weapon was proximity; these were the gods who hid in plain sight.

The Israelites lived in a place where diversity prevailed, much like in our society. There were many people groups and many different gods. The dominant deity was Baal, whose name meant "owner, master, lord." Sound familiar? Baal had started his career as a god of weather, but expanded into fertility and, from there, to such things as ritual prostitution.

There was also a mother goddess, Ashtoreth. The sacrifices, the temples, the sexual rituals — these things enticed the Israelites. And the prophets of the Old Testament despised them above all other gods.[10] Why? Because these gods had the home field advantage. They were right there.

Two of the most significant factors that determine which gods win the war are *time* and *place*. We may be not confronting Baal or Ashtoreth. But we struggle with the gods of our culture every day. Fertility rituals and temple prostitution are easy for us to reject, because they don't fit in with our times. But could it be that we have our own idols that hide in plain sight, that we don't recognize simply because they're so common? Maybe it's the gods of fame, materialism, or appearance.

Paul writes, "Do not conform to the pattern of this world, but be transformed by the renewing of your mind" (Romans 12:2). "The pattern of this world" is his way of describing the spirit, or the gods, of this age. To go with the flow is to conform to the pattern of this world. J. B. Phillips paraphrased that verse, "Don't let the world around you squeeze you into its own mould."

The Bible advises us to renew our minds by plugging them into the eternal, unchanging truth of the one God.

God Himself

But as for me and my household, we will serve the Lord.
— Joshua 24:15

This brings us to Joshua's fourth option — the Lord God. The final option, of course, has really been the only good option all along. After all, none of the other options are even real. They are nothing more than mirages. They may look promising, but they do nothing to satisfy our thirst.

Before Joshua gives the people these four options, he stacks the deck just a bit by describing all the things God has done for his people over the years. The Lord God had been active and worked powerfully among them — redeeming, protecting, guiding, and providing. So in making a choice, the obvious question for the people to ask these other gods was, *What have you ever done for us?*

In making your own choice, I would recommend you ask yourself the same. What enduring value has the god of wealth really bought anyone? Did the gods of pleasure ever once deliver true and lasting happiness? What about the gods of sex? Can they provide a joy that is more than a passing moment?

What have these gods done for us? If anything, they have enslaved us. They have robbed us. They have disappointed us.

Tom Brady was asked that question. If you follow football, you'll know that he is the quarterback for the New England Patriots. He's a superstar, a guy with three Super Bowl rings. He holds pages of passing records, earned nearly $40 million in 2013, and has dated a succession of supermodels — eventually marrying one of them. By every standard of this world, he has it going on.

That's why we're so surprised to hear his interview on TV's *60 Minutes*. He asked Steve Kroft, the interviewer, "Why do I have three Super Bowl rings and still think there's something greater out there for me? I mean, maybe a lot of people would say, 'Hey man, this is what [it's all about].' I reached my goal, my dream, my life. Me? I think, 'It's got to be more than this.' I mean this isn't — this can't be — all it's cracked up to be."

When Kroft asked him what "the answer" might possibly be, Brady replied, "What's the answer? I wish I knew. I love playing football, and I love being quarterback for this team. But at the same time, I think there are a lot of other parts about me that I'm trying to find."[11]

Brady is honest and even wise. He knows that a great chunk of the world admires him. He also knows that wealth, fame, power, pleasure, and accomplishment don't provide the ultimate prize in life. He has asked himself, *What have those gods done for me?* And he has to answer with courageous frankness, "Not enough."

Yet I know people, and you do too, who point to invisible,

intangible things when they discuss the meaning of life. They are followers of Jesus Christ, and if you ask them what he has done for them, you'll hear words like forgiveness, fulfillment, hope, joy, and peace. Psalm 86:8 puts it this way: "Among the gods there is none like you, Lord; no deeds can compare with yours."

Back to Joshua. How do the people respond to his great four-way challenge?

They say exactly the right words. "Then the people answered, 'Far be it from us to forsake the Lord to serve other gods! It was the Lord our God himself who brought us and our parents up out of Egypt, from that land of slavery, and performed those great signs before our eyes. He protected us on our entire journey and among all the nations through which we traveled. And the Lord drove out before us all the nations, including the Amorites, who lived in the land. We too will serve the Lord, because he is our God'" (Joshua 24:16 – 18).

We would expect Joshua to say, "That's what I'm talking about!" Or perhaps something more formal, such as, "You have chosen well!" But oddly, he doesn't let them off the hook so easily. Joshua begins to talk about the jealousy of God, the holiness of God. He describes the disaster that will come upon them if they don't live up to the words they're speaking.

Joshua, you see, is an old man. He has watched these people all his life. He knows how fickle their hearts are, how quickly their attention wanders. He knows how easily they say the right things, only to turn around and make the wrong choices. And so a warning is issued.

This story has a cautionary ending. It comes only two Bible chapters after the one we've been reading. "Joshua son of Nun, the servant of the Lord, died at the age of a hundred and ten. And they buried him in the land of his inheritance, at Timnath Heres in the hill country of Ephraim, north of Mount Gaash. After that whole generation had been gathered to their ancestors, *another generation grew up who knew neither the Lord nor what he had done for Israel"* (Judges 2:8 – 10, emphasis added).

We've said it more than once: the gods never surrender. They may lose a generation, but even then they say, "We'll get the next one." They may lose you for a day, but they'll be back tomorrow.

Idol ID

We are all wired for worship, and our choices are a strong indication of what gods we are worshiping.

What I decide I want to do for a living.

How I choose to spend my money.

What I choose to watch on TV.

The people I choose to have as friends.

The websites I choose to visit.

The clothes I choose to wear.

The way I choose to spend my free time.

What I choose to think about.

All of these choices reveal my god of choice.

So instead of me asking you about what gods you are worshiping, let me ask you about what choices you are making. Stop for a moment and consider your options, and then choose carefully.

How close are your choices to those of your parents?
Consider those things you will do or decide this week. How many of them reflect the thinking and values of your parents? Do you have similar opinions on major things happening in the world? Do you pursue the same goals? Do you sacrifice for the same things? Is it possible that you

are worshiping the same "gods beyond the river" that your parents worship?

What gods and goals have you inherited without really realizing it?

If you have chosen to worship the Lord God, how much of that is your parents' decision, and how much is your own?

What gods would you identify as the "gods of culture"?
Perhaps this is the question that requires the most demanding reflection, because these gods are often such a part of our daily lives that we don't recognize them. But take a moment and look at the world around you through the lens of idolatry. Can you recognize the true American idols?

Think of two or three movies or television shows you've watched recently. Bring to mind a few of the songs you listened to today. What is held up and pursued? What are the gods that our culture glorifies and honors?

How has following Christ impacted your choices?
If you are a follower of Jesus, how do your choices differ from those of your parents, your friends, and your culture?

Do you approach money and possessions differently than your parents? Than your best friends?

Have your priorities or pursuits changed since you started following Jesus? Are you still living for the same things?

What choices have you made that go against cultural ideals because you are a follower of Jesus? Is there anything about your dating life or entertainment choices that sets you apart from the world?

What priorities and pursuits continue to influence you?
Is there something or someone from your past that takes the place of the Lord God in your life? A god that you were living for? What stuff is on the bottom of your shoes? What gods from your past continue to war for the throne of your heart? What do you need to leave behind in order to follow Jesus more completely?

part 2

the temple of
pleasure

Have you ever thought about the place of pleasure in modern life? I'm talking about the plain old pursuit of fun in all its forms.

There have always been games, stories, jokes, and songs, but today pleasure is something close to the theme of daily living. We even expect school and our daily responsibilities to be pleasurable. That's not how our ancestors looked at things. In a society based on agriculture, nobody said, "Know what? Plowing and tending cattle aren't enough fun for me."

But these days if it isn't fun, we don't want to do it. We have more leisure time and more money to spend. And how much do we spend? Well, it depends on what kinds of things you specify as part of the "pleasure industry."

We know this much: People spend trillions of dollars each year trying to make themselves happy, whether it's with various forms of entertainment, with drugs or drink, or with one of the countless other items that promise to turn your frown upside down.

In a postindustrial society, our survival needs are met. We sold the farm, after all, and we've gathered in cities where we have food, shelter, plenty of water, and a surplus of time.

I know what you're thinking: *No one has a surplus of time. I'm busier than ever.* Fair enough, but what are we busy doing? Quite often, the answer is chasing pleasure.

When we experience pleasure, there's a part of us that thinks, *Yes! This is what I was made for.* Even if you haven't experienced much pleasure in your life, you've experienced enough to know that you want more. Thus begins the quest for the elusive narcotic of pleasure.

And so the gods of pleasure whisper, "Wouldn't you like to scratch that itch? Wouldn't you like to satisfy that appetite? Wouldn't you like to experience that feeling? Wouldn't you like to get that high? I have what you are looking for right here."

And so we walk into the temple of pleasure. And there we see the gods of drugs, sex, and entertainment. There are others, to be sure, but these are the ones we most often find ourselves bowing down to, making what on the surface are good gifts from God into something that draws our heart away from him. And when we begin to worship pleasure, the end result is always pain.

Just to be clear, I want to say right from the start that food, sex, and entertainment are not sinful or evil in and of themselves. In fact these things all have the potential to be good gifts from God that draw our hearts to him all the more. But inside the temple of pleasure, gifts are turned into gods.

Remember Joshua's impassioned speech to the people challenging them to choose which god they would serve? The people chose the Lord God, and they were told to throw away the gods of the Egyptians.

But instead of destroying the old gods, they put them in storage. Several hundred years pass, and the nation of Israel splits into the northern kingdom and the southern kingdom. The first king of the northern kingdom is Jeroboam, and he doesn't want his people going to Jerusalem in the southern kingdom to worship God. Besides making his own gods, he also decides to grab the keys to the storage unit and pull out the gods of the Egyptians for the people to worship.

The worship of these idols continues as the kings come and go. Then a man named Ahab, son of Omri, ascends to the throne of Israel. And we read that he "did more evil in the eyes of the Lord than any of those before him" (1 Kings 16:30).

This king marries a woman named Jezebel, whose name is still in the dictionary as another word for "an immoral or manipulative woman." She sets up an altar and a temple for the god of Baal in Samaria.

Jezebel has many prophets of the true God killed — and God, as we have seen, is jealous. He reaches the point where he has had enough of the people's unfaithfulness and he sends his prophet Elijah to Ahab. Elijah says to the king, "As the Lord, the God of Israel, lives, whom I serve, there will be neither dew nor rain in the next few years except at my word" (1 Kings 17:1).

Save your bottled water — a drought is coming.

Please understand that weather is Baal's thing. His number one talent, supposedly, is taking care of meteorological issues. This is why the genuine God withholds rain. It's the most obvious way to get the attention of unfaithful people.

God withholds his blessing in the very areas in which we lift up false gods.

For example, has anyone noticed any significant economic problems in our money-obsessed culture lately?

How about problems with drugs — abuses of over-the-counter drugs, performance enhancers, and marijuana and alcohol?

What about sex? You can't escape it in our overly sexualized culture.

How about the entertainment industry? Isn't it interesting that one of the most common complaints of our entertainment-saturated society is boredom?

We shouldn't be surprised. After all, why would the Lord God bless us in the area that represents his greatest competition? So ask yourself: Is it possible that you're seeing a relationship drought, a contentment drought, or some other kind of challenge, because you want it so bad that it has become a god?

I'm not saying that's always the case, but you shouldn't expect God to help you down the path of chasing after an idol. He's not going to bless the one area of your life that is robbing him of his place on the throne of your heart. Why would God bless his primary competition?

Like Joshua, Elijah demands that the people stand, define the choice for what it is, and name their path: "Elijah went before the people and said, 'How long will you waver between two opinions? If the Lord is God, follow him; but if Baal is God, follow him.' But the people said nothing" (1 Kings 18:21).

It's a passage that is strikingly similar to Joshua 24, with the exception that the people are silent this time. Why? Could it be that, in the midst of a drought, they didn't want to make that choice? That they wanted to have it both ways?

They wanted to be followers of the Lord God, but they also wanted to be followers of Baal — after all, there was a drought in the land and they needed to cover all the bases. They wanted both, and so they said nothing.

As we look at these gods of pleasure in the next section of this book, I think you will find that the same is true of us. When forced to choose between the Lord God and the god of pleasure, we say nothing. Why? Because we want both.

the god
of the quick fix

Owen Mitchell grew up in farm country. Nearly every plant thrived in the fertile ground of his family farm: corn, soybeans, alfalfa. Rows of crops grew in neat lines in irrigated fields. But with abundant plant life came numerous weeds, including one particular *weed*. Call it marijuana, reefer, pot, dope, chronic, or ganja — it grew wild on the borders of well-tended fields.

Owen didn't pay much attention to the weeds as a child. But when he got into high school, he started to take notice and think about lighting up. Football injuries, stressful classes, and lots of free time with nothing to do finally led him to "harvest" some of the plants. He and his friends would smoke the weed behind the barn or under the bleachers at the football field.

It's no worse than smoking cigarettes, Owen thought. *Besides, I'm not hurting anyone but myself.*

Owen enjoyed the mellow feeling that pot gave him. His stresses diminished. His problems felt smaller.* But so did his dreams. It didn't take long for Owen's grades to drop. His plans for life shrunk, as did his desire to go to college.

With his parents pushing him to get off the farm, he did end up making it into a state university. As an undeclared freshman, Owen figured he'd get some general education requirements out

---

* As did the contents of his wallet. All of those munchies cost a lot of money.

of the way, get his act together, and figure out what he wanted to do with his life. He could give up smoking weed anytime he wanted; he wasn't so sure he could say the same thing about the cigarettes he'd started lighting up.

The hunger for the drugs, however, didn't go away so easily. The god of the quick fix who had provided him comfort, security, and confidence bided his time. Very soon, this god would counterattack.

Comfort Drug

After years of decline, pot smoking among teens and college students has grown in the last five years. (Maybe you've noticed it yourself.) Your peers give a lot of reasons for their desire to experiment with drugs or alcohol. Sure, some just want to fit in. Others eventually cave in to pressure. But the top responses as to why people your age try drugs are nearly always the same: to escape problems and relieve stress.

Though hard drug use tends to get a lot of focus, it's not the only tool this god has at his disposal to help you feel a little better. He whispers the party you're at is only better now that there's alcohol, and holding that red cup will help you relax and fit in. And that sneaking a drink whenever you need one isn't a big deal. After all, this drug is perfectly legal, right, and possibly even already in your home. If you aren't interested in those options, it doesn't faze him; he points to an entire store down the street ready to provide all the cheese-dusted, new-and-improved Value-Sized happiness you desire. And this option is probably even on sale.*

Food, in fact, might be this god's real secret weapon. According to the American Center for Disease Control, 68 percent of Americans are overweight, and one-third of Americans are obese.

---

*Not to mention the special coupon savings.

But the scales don't tell the whole story, do they? You could happen to have a strong metabolism and look very fit, but food could still be a god you look to. Or you might focus your life on organic, healthy foods, and still be building your life around a false god albeit a healthier one. And this granola version has another side — he gets you to focus on your appearance in order to feel good. In other words, to worship your own image.

I feel like I need to make something clear at this point. There is nothing wrong with taking prescription drugs to treat a condition or illness. It's not idolatry to receive competent medical care. There's also nothing wrong with food itself — God created it to taste good, and even gave us ten thousand taste buds in order to enjoy it. The problem comes when we start to look to drugs — prescription and otherwise — or food to do for us what the Lord God alone should do.

Why would we do that? Well, maybe the day brought its share of disappointments. Maybe you didn't receive the place on the team you were hoping for; maybe you had to endure another snarky post from a classmate on your Tumblr or Facebook page; maybe school itself has become hard to face. Maybe it's family issues, and the thought of going home makes school seem like a day at the beach.

Instead of turning to God, how often do we turn to something else? We rant at a friend. Open up a quart of Blue Bell Pralines and Cream ice cream.* Or in some cases, sneak a drink from a parent's liquor bottle or go to a friend's house to get high.

When the going gets tough, the tough get toking, or drinking, or chowing down. Drugs provide a quick and obvious shot of comfort. Over twenty states have legalized "medical" uses of marijuana. If you go to some beaches in California, you'll find medical marijuana shops on every corner with signs out front, saying "The

---

* Just a random example.

Doctor Is In."* Colorado and Washington have even legalized the use of recreational pot. Alcohol and other drugs promise to make you feel better. The food lovingly prepared by a relative or poured from a crinkling bag promises to fill a hole. And they do—for a brief time.

But no matter the method we choose, the god of the quick fix demands a high price once it's seated on the throne of your life.

Think about this: Comforter is one of the names God calls himself. He is the God of all comfort and he is ready to talk with you about your day. The Prince of Peace waits to give you his gifts and strengthen you. He wants to be your satisfaction and show you compassion. Second Corinthians 1:3–4 says, "Praise be to the God and Father of our Lord Jesus Christ, the Father of compassion and the God of all comfort, who comforts us in all our troubles, so that we can comfort those in any trouble with the comfort we ourselves have received from God."

STUCK IN THE WEEDS

Some people argue that a bunch of leaves can't be harmful, right? Wrong.

Marijuana has a chemical in it called delta–9-tetrahydocannabinol, better known as THC. About four hundred other chemicals can be found in marijuana as well. But THC is up to no good in your brain. It has been proven to interfere with learning and memory. A recent study followed people from age thirteen to thirty-eight. Those who used marijuana in their teens had a significant drop in their IQ, even if they quit later in life. People who use marijuana over the long term report less life satisfaction, poorer education and job achievement, and more personal problems compared to those who do not

---

*If you consider a guy in dreadlocks and a tie-dyed lab coat a doctor.

try pot. Marijuana may also increase your risk of developing psychosis, depression, and anxiety.

But marijuana isn't addictive, right? Wrong again.

One in six people who start smoking marijuana at a young age become addicted to the drug. In addition, marijuana usage may lead to dangerous experimentation with other drugs.

"The nation's teenage drug problems are far from disappearing," says Dr. Lloyd Johnston of the University of Michigan. "We continue to see a number of new drugs coming onto the scene, like synthetic marijuana and 'bath salts.' Synthetic drugs like these are particularly dangerous, because they have unknown, untested, and ever-changing ingredients that can be unusually powerful, leading to severe consequences. Users really don't know what they are getting and, as the thousands of calls to the nation's poison control centers relating to these drugs indicate, they may be in for a very unpleasant surprise."

Statistics from National Institute on Drug Abuse for Teens, "The Science Behind Drug Abuse: Drug Facts, Marijuana, http://teens.drugabuse.gov/drug-facts/marijuana (accessed October 10, 2013). Dr. Lloyd Johnson quote from "Rise in Teen Marijuana Use Stalls," Institute for Social Research at the University of Michigan, December 18, 2012, http://home.isr.umich.edu/releases/rise-in-teen-marijuana-use-stalls/ (accessed October 10, 2013).

A Different Kind of Drunkenness

Paul played a huge role in the spread of Christianity in the early church. His efforts are still felt today, as much of the New Testament is a reproduction of letters that he wrote to various people and churches. We know him best as the apostle Paul.

In the book of Ephesians, Paul writes to new Gentile (non-Jewish) believers at a church in Turkey. He wants to encourage them by saying that they're part of Christ's body and also explain God's moral laws, which they aren't following or may not know about. In chapter five, Paul begins by encouraging them as beloved children to follow God's example. He tells them that there should be no hint of sexual immorality—a big problem in their day and ours (but more on that in the next chapter). And then, implores them to "be very careful, then, how you live—not as unwise but as wise," and he adds, "Do not get drunk on wine, which leads to debauchery. Instead, be filled with the Spirit" (Ephesians 5:15, 18).

Debauchery is just a fancy way of saying bad or immoral behavior. Getting drunk or getting high leads to debauchery. You lose self-control. Your inhibitions go away and you end up doing things and making decisions that you never would if you were sober. And many times these decisions lead to feelings of guilt, shame, and embarrassment once the buzz wears off.

Instead of getting drunk (and if he were writing today, he would probably add "high"), Paul gives us a better alternative. He tells us to be filled with the Spirit. Some people have even called it being drunk in the Spirit. Paul knows that by filling our lives with God's presence and following his will we'll be so joyful, content, and happy that we'll have no need for drugs or alcohol, or even a focus on food. When it comes to most things in life, moderation is the key. We shouldn't eat too much, drink too much, exercise constantly, stare at a screen too much, or play video games for hours. But when it comes to our relationship with God, too much is never enough.

He doesn't want us to dip our toe in the pool. God wants us to cannonball into the deep end of our faith. He wants to surround our lives with his love and sit alone on the throne of our hearts.

Owen More to Drugs

For Owen, university life in the big city brought even more temptations than his rural upbringing. There were parties, frat houses, bars, girls, and different types of drugs. He didn't make it through two years of college before dropping out.

He married at twenty and went into sales to support his family. His engaging personality made it easy for him to sell anything — cars, insurance, even the marijuana that he grew in his basement. Pretty soon he connected with other drug dealers.

Maybe you've heard marijuana called the "gateway drug" because it can lead to trying harder, more dangerous drugs. Well, that was the case for Owen. To relieve the stresses of family life and a mortgage, Owen began sniffing cocaine and trying a cocktail of other drugs. It didn't take long before drugs sat in the center of his life, pushing family, friends, and everything else aside.

His wife divorced him, taking the kids. Sinking deeper into drugs, Owen began selling harder drugs to support his addiction. His friends got more dangerous. His customer base grew, and he even began selling to undercover police officers.

One morning, Owen woke up with his house surrounded by law enforcement officials with their guns drawn. He was taken from his house, convicted, and sent to prison.

This wasn't the life this once-innocent farm boy had envisioned for himself. He regretted trying that first "weed" out in the field and wanted a new start.

Owen discovered that his life could have exactly that when a chaplain visited him in prison. The chaplain didn't sugarcoat Owen's poor decisions, but explained that Jesus Christ offered forgiveness to all who gave their hearts fully to him. Past mistakes would be forgotten. Sins would be washed whiter than snow.

He believed God's promise and accepted Jesus' sacrifice for the atonement of his sins. The god of the quick fix was dethroned. This god had promised stress relief and fun, but only provided misery, heartache, and problems. Owen knew he had a long way to go. But he felt a peace and hope that'd he'd always longed for. Jesus was finally at his rightful place on the throne of his life.

God cannot and will not give us a sense of lasting pleasure

apart from him, because it violates his purpose and our design. Psalm 34:8 reads, "Taste and see that the Lord is good."

Drink that down the next time this god calls out to you. And just say no.

If you're already addicted to having the god of the quick fix on the throne of your heart, you may have to seek professional help to knock this modern-day false god out of your life. There's nothing embarrassing about admitting that you can't defeat this god on your own. If you've hidden this god from your parents, tell them about your addiction. Let your youth pastor know and ask for prayer and accountability. You may even want to speak to a counselor or check in to a treatment center. The god of the quick fix is one of the most difficult to dethrone, because it's so easy to take your problems away, and it feels good to do so. But it can be conquered. Admit your addiction and seek help.

It honors the one true God and it honors yourself as his child when you get the help you need in defeating this false god. God used Paul in mighty ways once he sat firmly in the throne of Paul's heart. And that's the same God we serve. He's a God of forgiveness, a God of compassion, a God of mercy, and a God of comfort. He can use our past mistakes to bring him glory and us comfort in the future.

Remember what 2 Corinthians 1:3 – 4 says: God is a compassion and comfort who comforts us in our troubles, "so that we can comfort those in any trouble with the comfort we ourselves have received from God." Once you defeat the god of the quick fix in your own life, God can use you to help others do the same. There's a power, hope, and comfort that can only come from the Lord when his love rules our hearts and defines our lives.

Idol ID

Do you take drugs for medical reasons/eat for sustenance or just to escape?

Take a look at your habits and discern why you turn to drugs or food. Is it mostly because of pleasure or to help with a medical problem? Again, there is nothing wrong about taking an Advil to get rid of a headache or enjoying a good hamburger; but when we turn to drugs or food to dull an ache in our heart, they have a way of expanding beyond their borders and taking over our lives.

In 1 Corinthians 10:31, Paul explains that instead of our daily comforts becoming an object of worship, we should give over everything we do as an act of worship to God. He wrote, "So whether you eat or drink or whatever you do, do it all for the glory of God."

When and why are you tempted to use drugs, alcohol, or food to fill a void?

How often do you buy into the concept of getting "comfortably numb"? Do you use it as a salve for daily wounds?

When life goes wrong, some people's first impulse is to turn to something quick and easy. Something often readily available, even, when applicable, to those who are underage.

Consider the times that you are tempted. Is it before a big test when you're trying to deal with life? Is it after everyone else is in bed and you decide to wind down? Is it with friends who have easy access to drugs or alcohol? Is it when you're feeling lonely, or even bored with life?

Would you be willing to stop your habit cold turkey?

One of the easiest ways to gauge the power that the god of

the quick fix has over you is to completely cut whatever it calls you to do out of your life. How hard would it be for you to stay away from drugs or alcohol or three days, one week, or even a month? To not stop at your favorite fast food place whenever you drive by, or grab a bag of chips in those times you need a pick-me-up or need to de-stress?

Don't do it as a test of discipline. Do it for the expressed purpose of spending time with God and committing to putting him back in his rightful place in your life. Pray that you will have greater desire for him than for the physical comforts of this world.

CHOOSING JESUS:

Jesus My Deliverer

*Idols are defeated not by being removed
but by being replaced.*

The god of the quick fix promised us comfort, but we came up empty. He invited us to consume until it consumed our lives. We tasted everything until nothing satisfied anymore.

And so finally we came to Jesus. We discovered that he offers us perfect peace and contentment. He fills our every need. Every hunger ultimately leads back to him.

David wrote, "The righteous cry out, and the LORD hears them; he delivers them from all their troubles" (Psalm 34:17).

Jesus frees us from an addictive, dysfunctional relationship with our temptations because he is our deliverer, and in him we discover what we were searching for all along. If we seek our peace in drugs, alcohol, or food, then the source of our comfort always disappears and always must be found again — a consumable god. A never-ending vicious circle that pulls us deeper and deeper into despair. It is different with Jesus.

Nothing feels better than the joy and satisfaction of knowing Christ. Nothing comforts the soul as he does. Nothing feeds and strengthens and renews us like the time we spend with him each day.

He bids us to take and eat. He bids us to come to the well where he offers living water, so that we never thirst again.

Think of a time when you've come in from the hot sun, drenched with sweat and with a parched throat, and downed a cool glass of ice water. Did anything ever taste better?

Such a moment is no more than a vague hint of what it feels like to be spiritually empty and find our deliverance in Jesus. The god of the quick fix promises freedom, but leads to a cage — maybe even a jail cell. Christ offers unbounded freedom and joy. Paul writes in 2 Corinthians 3:17, "Now the Lord is the Spirit, and where the Spirit of the Lord is, there is freedom."

Drink deep in the spirit. Get drunk from his living water. It is only when we find our comfort in Christ and he takes the throne of our lives that we understand what true peace and freedom feels like.

the god
of sex

Sex is good.

I just want to be real clear about that up front.

In fact, sex is a gift from God himself. But isn't it amazing how some of the richest and most beautiful gifts from God are often the same gifts that are twisted into hideous and destructive idols?

Sex was God's idea. He designed it to intimately connect a man and woman in a marriage relationship. Sex, done God's way, can create a supernatural bond between us. At the creation of humanity, it was arranged by God that "a man leaves his father and mother and is joined to his wife, and the two are united into one" (Genesis 2:24 NLT).

This is a spiritual union that is captured and reflected in the physical act of making love. One of the Hebrew words for sex, translated literally, is "a mingling of the souls," and that captures it perfectly — a beautiful gift from God.

It brings pleasure and intimacy and, of course, produces children, in accordance with God's plan. He could have made reproduction a simple, mechanical, joyless act of natural instinct. He could have created sex to feel the same way it feels when your hair grows. But he chose to make it pleasurable.

God is a father who likes to give his children good things.

All his gifts point us back to him. Or at least that's how it should work. The gift should cause us to love and worship the giver more deeply. But all too easily God's gifts to us end up being his greatest competition.

This is what happens all too frequently with sex.

It is beautiful until it loses its spiritual context. Pleasures can be wonderful until they become ends in themselves. They become gods, and the gods become tyrants, and the tyrants become slave masters.

A Fairy Tale Gone Wrong

There's an old story about a prince and a princess. But this one is unlike stories found in picture books, and Disney is unlikely to create an animated feature film about it. It's told in the Bible in 2 Samuel 13, and it's a true story.

David, the king of Israel, in keeping with the custom of his time, had many wives and many children by them. It's worth noting that, far from approving or even condoning polygamy, the Old Testament provides one example after another of why it doesn't work.

The main characters are Amnon, one of David's sons, a prince of Israel, and Tamar, David's daughter by a different wife, a princess of Israel. The Bible says, "Amnon became so obsessed with his sister Tamar that he made himself ill" (2 Samuel 13:2).

Amnon constantly thought about and focused on one image in his mind. He allowed this fantasy to fill his heart until he made himself sick with lust.

Amnon had a friend and advisor who wanted to know why the prince was looking so rough. Amnon explained that he couldn't get the thought of being with Tamar out of his mind. The advisor gave him the following advice: "Okay, Amnon, here's what you do. Call in sick to the palace today. Then your dad, the king, will be worried, and he'll come to check up on you. You tell him that it would really help your recovery if your sister Tamar were to come in and bake you some of her homemade bread. When she comes in, you'll tell her you just love to watch her cook. Then, my man, I think you can take it from there, right?"*

Amnon went with it. When his half sister came in to cook for him, he said to her, "Tell the servants we won't be needing them this evening." Then he instructed her to come to the bedroom and feed him the bread.

What happened next is heartbreaking. He pushed the food aside and declared what was on his mind. She resisted. She pled for him to think about what he was doing, to think about the disgrace it would inflict upon her and his own reputation.

The Bible says, "But he refused to listen to her, and since he was stronger than she, he raped her" (2 Samuel 13:14).

Tamar did what the people of her time did to demonstrate great mourning and suffering. She put ashes on her head and tore the beautiful robe she was wearing. These actions also symbolized her loss of virginity. She left weeping and broken.

Amnon's sexual sin brought incredible destruction and devastation, not just upon his family but on the entire nation. The disruption to a royal family means disruption to a country. Everything spiraled wildly out of control.

And where did it all begin? It began with idolatry. Amnon chose to worship the god of sexual pleasure. He spent countless hours lusting after Tamar until it became his obsession.

I know what you're thinking: *What in the world does this story have to do with me? I would never go down that path and commit such a heinous act.* But that's exactly the kind of thing Amnon probably said to himself before this happened. The god of sex specializes in taking you further than you ever intended to go.

So let me ask you, have the thoughts, or even pursuit, of sexual pleasure become an obsession? Is it the last thing you think about

---

*I'm paraphrasing, but that's pretty much how it went down.

at night and the first thing that comes to mind in the morning? Do you daydream about it at school, risk your reputation, friendships, and relationships for it?

Do you feel the presence of God fading into a cloud of deepening shame?

The Pleasure Paradox

When something good becomes a god, the pleasure it brings dies in the process. Pleasure has this unique trait: The more intensely you chase it, the less likely you are to catch it.

Philosophers call this the "hedonistic paradox." The idea is that pleasure, pursued for its own sake, evaporates before our eyes.

The Bible records how Amnon responded when he finally gave in to his lust. It didn't satisfy him the way he thought it would. Just the opposite happened. The incident lasted just a matter of moments, and when it was over Amnon looked at Tamar with contempt, even with "intense hatred."

According to the Scriptures, "He hated her more than he had loved her" (2 Samuel 13:15).

What a strange verse. "He hated her more than he had loved her." What does that mean? She didn't do anything to him. It doesn't make any sense.

But I'm guessing some of you have an idea about what's going on here. The god of sexual pleasure promises you incredible satisfaction. As you surf websites and watch videos, as you keep going a little bit farther with your boyfriend or girlfriend, you obsess over what it would be like to push the envelope, to go ahead and give in to your desires, to grab that moment of ecstasy.

But what happens? The god delivers the opposite of what is promised.

Instead of satisfaction, you experience emptiness and an almost immediate hunger for something more. Instead of closeness and intimacy, you experience a strange sense of loneliness.

COUNTING THE COST

In our sexually saturated society, it's nearly impossible to avoid pornography. A survey of fifteen- and seventeen-year-old Internet users discovered that seven out of ten "accidentally" viewed pornography very or somewhat often. And when a group of teenagers were studied for a year, nearly all of them viewed pornographic images. (Among fifteen-year-olds it was 98.9 percent of boys and 73.5 percent of girls.)

Instead of a quick thrill and passing sexual rush, researchers have discovered that viewing pornography can have long-term effects:

- A greater tendency toward sexually aggressive behaviors, including sexual assault, sexual harassment, and rape.

- A decrease in how much one values faithfulness. Sex outside marriage begins to seem less forbidden, more of a real option.

- A major increase in sex without attachment. Sex becomes a physical act, rather than an intimate connection. It isolates instead of bonds people.*

---

*"The Impact of Pornography on Children and Youth," January 14, 2011, http://www.preventtogether.org/Resource (accessed October 12, 2013).

You think that the steak will match the sizzle, that it all will pay off, that you will feel complete. Instead, you can't shake the impression that you've given away some part of yourself that you can't get back.

When the gift replaces the giver as the object of our worship, something surprising happens. When we begin to worship this god of pleasure instead of the God who gave it to us, we discover that much of the pleasure is lost. We discover the devastating fact that when we pursue pleasure as a god, pleasure disappears.

The Morning After

Let's go back to our story of Elijah. The drought had brought devastation to the land. Elijah goes to King Ahab and sets up what amounts to a cage match between the Lord God and the gods of Baal and Asherah. People from all over Israel gather on Mount Carmel to watch the "battle of the gods." On one side is Elijah, representing the Lord. On the other side stand 850 prophets representing the false gods. Elijah says to the 850 prophets:

> "Choose one of the bulls and prepare it first, since there are so many of you. Call on the name of your god, but do not light the fire." So they took the bull given them and prepared it.
>
> Then they called on the name of Baal from morning till noon. "Baal, answer us!" they shouted. But there was no response; no one answered. And they danced around the altar they had made.
>
> At noon Elijah began to taunt them. "Shout louder!" he said. "Surely he is a god! Perhaps he is deep in thought, or busy* or traveling. Maybe he is sleeping and must be awakened." So they shouted louder and slashed themselves with swords and spears, as was their custom, until their blood flowed.
>
> — 1 Kings 18:25 – 28

What a sight it must have been. These prophets are cutting and slashing themselves, desperate to get the attention of their god. We shake our heads at the ridiculousness of such behavior. They worship their false god with greater and greater intensity, thinking

---

*The translation for the word *busy* is "Maybe he's relieving himself." Seriously.

that if they just give a little more, then their god will respond. This all seems so primitive. How can it be relevant to us today?

But have we not bled upon the altar of sexual pleasure?

Some have sacrificed their finances. More money is spent on pornography in this country every year than on rock music, country music, jazz, and classical music put together. More money is spent on pornography than pro baseball, basketball, and football combined. Last year it grossed more than ABC, NBC, CBS, and FOX combined. It's an industry worth more than $10 billion annually.

But it's not just our money we've sacrificed to this god. Many adults have sacrificed their marriages, their children, and their careers on its altar.

As a pastor I have had many men, and increasingly women, come to me and talk about their addiction to pornography. I look into their eyes and see what this cruel god has required of them. I see how they have slashed at themselves until they are weak and miserable.

I've talked to men and women who are in bondage to extramarital affairs. It started with flattering remarks from a coworker — a little smile here, a suggestion there, a friend request is accepted. Now their marriages are destroyed.

I've had students like you write to me, telling me how online images that used to disgust them are now the very images they require for arousal. They don't know who they are becoming or where it will all lead. They have so much despair and fear for their futures.

"It's just looking at pictures," we say. "It's harmless entertainment."

No. It's really not. It's a form of worship. It's the laying of our souls on an altar before a god who only wants to consume us. You are giving your heart to this god, and everything flows from the heart. Eventually the garbage makes its way downstream and comes to the surface.

It may look different than it did back then, but make no mistake about it: We shout, dance, and eventually bleed for this god, hoping for some kind of response. But the god of sexual pleasure always demands more.

In Romans 6:19, Paul describes sin as "ever-increasing." It happens with drugs. It happens with pornography or the need for money. The gods keep demanding more. It's what is called the law of diminishing returns. Pleasure is always being promised around the next corner, after the next mile or the next sacrifice of your values. But the sacrifices cut deeper, and the satisfaction becomes more fleeting. "Midday passed, and they continued their frantic prophesying until the time for the evening sacrifice. But there was no response, no one answered, no one paid attention" (1 Kings 18:29).

There is no response. One of the saddest parts of my job is seeing people spend their lives worshiping a god that takes away everything and leaves them with nothing. I don't want that to be your future.

Roadways of the Mind

I'm sure that on the first day Amnon noticed Tamar's beauty and lusted after her it seemed harmless enough. After all, it wasn't like he was going to act on his feelings. It was just...thinking. The battlefield of the gods is your heart. Your heart is shaped by your thoughts. Your thoughts determine who will win the throne for your heart. Proverbs 4:23 reads, "Above all else, guard your heart, for everything you do flows from it."

Let me reword that for you: Be careful how you think, because that's what you will worship. That's why the Bible tells us to take every thought captive. What you think about ultimately has a lot to do with which god will win the war.

The battle begins in your mind, and it's not only the Bible that tells us so. Psychologists have provided increasing insight as to how that happens. During the last few decades, for example, the dominant movement in their field is what we call cognitive psychology. It examines how our thoughts shape our attitudes, emotions, and behavior.

Thoughts, attitudes, and emotions are all intertwined, but the mind is the starting point. Think about how much effort it takes to carve a path through the woods. It's tiring and challenging. You cut out bushes, vines, and saplings, and the path is barely visible. But then people begin to use your path. The ground becomes a well-trodden trail that looks as if it's been there forever.

Scientists tell us the brain works the same way. A new thought is like a blazed trail, and it's actually called a neural pathway. Right now your brain is pushing back the wilderness of your still-shifting mind, creating these roads of thought. The subject of sex is strange and challenging on first hearing, but then all the traffic of movies, music, reality TV, and school conversations twists the pathways into various parts of the woods.

Imagine you are a young woman whose neural pathways have been worn down by ideas that her value is established by the appearance of her body, the shape of this, the size of that. You begin to dress and to apply makeup based upon thousands of messages that you need to have a certain kind of appeal — that, as a young woman, this is who you are.

Imagine you are a young man who has laid down his own mental highways. You end up viewing pornography, and that particular neural pathway becomes the main road. In time, it's the default route for any thought about the girls you meet. And lustful thinking only reinforces those roads.

I've heard one psychologist explain that lust and self-pleasure are playing with neurochemical fire. He says that it results in a narcissistic and selfish approach to sexuality in which we bind ourselves to ourselves (if that makes any sense). Sexuality is meant to be relationship-based, not a private and selfish experience.

I read about a study in which a man sat and viewed pornographic images for a certain period of time each day with a baseball cap on top of his computer monitor. After enough time went by, he could be sexually aroused by the sight of a baseball cap. So the question is, Who or what am I binding myself to? What roads am I building or reinforcing in my mind? And where will those roads lead me?

This is why idolatry is so dangerous. Our thoughts, our attitudes, and eventually our actions are determined by what we worship.

If you believe you can lock away your sexual thoughts in a special, airtight compartment, you've been taken in by a lie. The Bible tells us that "as he thinks in his heart, so is he" (Proverbs 23:7 NKJV). The mind determines who we are and who we are becoming. We think based on what we see and hear. So what are you feeding your mind?

We're told to "take captive every thought to make it obedient to Christ" (2 Corinthians 10:5). I love that metaphor of taking prisoners, because it's exactly what happens to our minds, one way or the other. We take it captive for truth or allow it to be seized and imprisoned by lies. Remember, this is war. The gods are at war for your soul.

If you've already started building a pornographic pathway through your mind, now is the time to change direction. Instead of trying to *not* think about sex — which may seem nearly impossible due to hormones and past images filling your brain — start thinking about the opposite sex in a positive, respectful way.

Instead of viewing people as sexual objects, see them as God's gift that completes you physically, emotionally, and sexually in a marriage relationship. Sure, you can appreciate their good looks, but focus more on their caring hearts, their fun personalities, and the fact that they're created by God. It is possible to retrain our brains and build new neural pathways, and in fact Paul gives great advice in Philippians 4:8: "Finally, brothers and sisters, whatever is true, whatever is noble, whatever is right, whatever is pure, whatever is lovely, whatever is admirable — if anything is excellent or praiseworthy — think about such things."

Whenever we look at the opposite sex, we should strive to see what is pure, lovely, admirable, true, right and excellent — not what is seedy and sexual.

Pleasure to Pain

When something good becomes a god, pleasure disappears and we experience pain.

Think through this with me. When we worship sex as a god, we find that it leads to the exact opposite of its divine design as a gift.

As a gift it brings connection; as a god it causes loneliness.

As a gift it brings pleasure; as a god it leads to emptiness.

As a gift it brings satisfaction; as a god it demands slavery.

As a gift it brings intimacy; as a god it creates separation.

As a gift it brings unity; as a god it often causes divorce.

It's a beautiful gift and a tyrant of a god.

The god of pleasure is the master of bait and switch, luring us in with images and promises that become the chains and shackles of our mental imprisonment.

Do you remember the first time you asked your parents for a pet? (Hang with me, there's a point to this story.) My oldest daughter was just four when she asked my wife and me; I agreed, but there were a few conditions.

First, the pet had to be something that didn't bark, meow, or make any kind of noise. Second, the pet couldn't shed any kind of fur or hair. Third, the pet had to cost less than five bucks.

Within those limitations, we finally settled on a goldfish. When we went to purchase the fish, the store offered a "three-day guarantee, no questions asked."

So we took the fish — him, her, who knows? — home with us. My daughter named it Nemo and was eager to play with her new pet. But how do you play with a fish? You can't take it for a walk. You can't teach it to fetch. But you can take it swimming.

So we put Nemo in a glass and took a trip to the swimming pool. Nemo swam in its cup at the edge of the pool while my daughter and I splashed in the water. Looking over I noticed that Nemo was watching us. I figured the fish longed to swim in the vast ocean of this swimming pool. But I explained to my daughter that chemicals in the pool might not be too good for Nemo. She was disappointed, but we moved on.

A while later, I was shocked to see that Nemo had moved on too. Nemo, living up to his name, had flip-flopped out of the cup and into the pool! I immediately started looking everywhere, trying to find Nemo. I spotted him in the deep end of the pool, living large and taking charge, darting back and forth. You could almost hear the theme music in the background. I knew I had to catch the little fish very quickly.

Have you ever tried catching a goldfish in a swimming pool? It's harder than it sounds.

All we could do was wait the fish out. Nemo swam more and more slowly until it floated to the surface — belly up.*

I feel Nemo's pain. The cup seemed so restrictive. Freedom looked so vast and enticing. And at first, once the fish dived in, it all felt so right. But what looked like pleasure was actually poison. The restriction turned out to be a loving thing, and "freedom" really meant destruction.

This is how the gods of pleasure work. What they offer is presented as freedom, but it's toxic once you make the plunge. They tell you there's no way you can be happy within the restraints God has set up. But the restraints are a design based on loving protection. The seat belt may cramp your style, and then save your life.

---

*I returned Nemo to the store later that day. The same lady who sold me the fish was still on duty, and even though the sign said, "No questions asked," she asked. I told her the truth: "The fish drowned."

The red traffic light makes you grumble, and then prevents a terrible collision. The gods of pleasure don't like traffic signals, seat belts, or moments of caution. They tell you to go for it.

Amnon would tell you to buckle up and slow down, because he discovered there wasn't any real or lasting pleasure in the god of sex. Just a quick release and then a whole lot of shame, pain, and emptiness. He had to have known his actions had consequences. Tamar told her full brother, Absalom, what had happened. Absalom burned with rage, but he waited for his moment. Notice that Absalom had an impulse to act on too; his happened to be a lust for revenge rather than sexual release. But he served a god that was just as destructive.

Absalom waited two years before finding the right opportunity to have Amnon assassinated in revenge for raping his sister. Then chaos reigned. King David, the father of these feuding sons, had to act, and it all boiled over into civil war. Absalom joined his half brother in the graveyard, and others died as well.

What if Amnon could've looked into the future and seen the results? On one side of the ledger would be a fleeting moment of sensual pleasure. On the other, his death, a civil war, and many lost lives. Why hadn't the whisper of lust included all of that?

Worship is powerful. It has huge consequences, whether you praise the God of heaven or the god of appetite. If you worship God, it changes everything about you and creates positive ripples that echo into eternity. If you worship false gods, the ripples bring a little of hell to earth.

When we worship the Lord God with this area of our lives, we experience what we were really wanting all long — deep and intimate pleasure. When we turn his gift of sex into a god, it's only a matter of time until it stops doing what it was designed to do. But when the gift causes us to worship the giver, we discover that the giver gives us his gifts all the more abundantly.

Idol ID

How well do you control your thought life?

One study shows that men think about sex nineteen times per day, and women ten.[12]

The thoughts will come, particularly in a highly sexualized society. You're not going to avoid being exposed to a barrage of suggestive imagery unless you move into a cave. The god of sexual pleasure has set up temples everywhere.

We need to take control of our thoughts, submitting them to God along with everything else in our lives. And we do have a great deal of control over what we do with those thoughts. When a thought comes, we must make a choice.

Take inventory of your thought life. What does it tell you about yourself? Ask God to make you more conscious of what's on your mind and to help you move your thinking in healthier directions. Remember Paul's advice in Philippians 4:8: "Finally, brothers and sisters, whatever is true, whatever is noble, whatever is right, whatever is pure, whatever is lovely, whatever is admirable — if anything is excellent or praiseworthy — think about such things."

The best way to keep the bad things out is to fill your mind up with the good things. In other words, we don't just remove the god of sexual pleasure. We replace the god of sex with the Lord God.

What sites do you visit on the Internet when you're by yourself?

Within two decades, the Internet has become the epicenter of our cultural sexual obsession. Think of the sites you visit as temples where you go to worship. This is another area over which we have control. Consider placing filters on your computer and smartphone, so that visiting questionable sites isn't even an option.

What might be lacking in your intimacy with God?
The real issue, of course, is a spiritual one. Sometimes people seek fantasies and pursuits of various kinds in an effort to fill a gap in their spirits. What is it we really need? What is it we think we're after when we chase fantasies?

Take inventory of where you stand with God these days. Is he real to you — a daily presence in your life? Where is he in your thoughts when the temptations come? Do you believe he has the power to rescue you?

Jesus taught his disciples to pray, "Lead us not into temptation, but deliver us from the evil one" (Matthew 6:13). Ask God to lead you to places and situations where you won't be tempted. Remember that he is always there, and will never leave you nor forsake you. Visualize his presence during the most trying moments. Draw near to God, and he will draw near to you.

The ultimate path away from a false god is the path toward the true one.

CHOOSING JESUS:

Jesus My Satisfaction

*Idols are defeated not by being removed
but by being replaced.*

The god of sex promised us satisfaction, yet he left us lonely and ashamed.

He lured and enticed us by distorting what was designed to be a gift and a blessing. He made it seem as if nothing could be more satisfying than the quick release of physical urges. Yet nothing could have left us feeling smaller and weaker — as if those urges defined who we were.

When we compare that to Jesus, who offers the greatest joy imaginable, we can see that the pursuit of the god of sex was never about love at all. It reduced the opposite sex to mere objects to be used for our personal pleasure. But the love of Jesus finds its greatest satisfaction in service rather than the servitude of others. It exalts them. It affirms them as children of God. It connects with them in body, soul, mind, and spirit.

Jesus is our satisfaction. All along, it was intimacy we really wanted, and he gives us that. When we have a love relationship with him, an unending honeymoon commences. Christ grows more wonderful to us every day.

Not that sex is put aside. On the contrary, it takes on a beauty we never could have imagined — the opposite of shame. We have been designed so that the level of intimacy we can have with our spouse is directly related to the depth of intimacy we have with Christ. Sexual intimacy as God designed it takes a human relationship to a whole new level, because we're not using one another; we're delighting in one another. The god of sex dehumanized us; Christ restores our wholeness and makes the two of us one flesh — so much the greater than the sum of our parts — as we seek him together.

The god of sex offers a counterfeit joy that becomes more elusive through time, ever harder to please, ever closer to emptiness. But the love of Christ only opens up to deeper joys, becoming ever greater.

Sexual pleasure, rightly viewed, is a rich gift that shows how much God loves us. But its ecstasy is only a foretaste of divine glory, a hint of the eternal pleasure of knowing, loving, and serving Christ. He is our true satisfaction.

the god
of entertainment

See if you can imagine this one.

People arrive hours early for church. On Sunday mornings, they don't just set a backup alarm on their cell phones to assure they wake up in time—they set a backup for the backup. Throughout the week, they talk about what happened the previous Sunday as excitement builds for the upcoming church service.

There are all-day radio talk shows devoted to reviewing last week's service and breaking down the next one. There's even a TV show called "ChurchCenter" that runs highlight clips of church activities that have happened across the nation.

When Sunday comes, the people load up their trucks, SUVs, and sedans hours before the service starts.

"Hurry," Dad says frantically. "We're behind again."

"It's 6:00 a.m." Mom says. "Church doesn't start for five hours."

"Last time we left at this time, we had to park three miles from the sanctuary and sit in the nosebleed seats. Someday, I really want to sit in the front row. But you have to camp out on the church lawn to have any chance of that."

The roads are really congested on the way to church, no matter how early you leave. At church, there are vehicles parked as far as the eye can see. Some members are tailgating, laying out elaborate spreads of barbequed meats on portable grills. Lawn chairs dot the church parking lot. Some people have television monitors and satellite dishes so they can catch updates from other worship services while they wait for their own to begin.

Even in the dead of winter, they'll be out here in the same numbers. And once the church doors open, the masses begin filing into the sanctuary, cheering with great passion and excitement. As the service starts, the people are all on their feet — not that they ever sit down. A bunch of young guys stand in the front row. None of them wears a shirt, but each one has a letter painted on his chest. Together they spell J-E-S-U-S.

After several hours of worship and an extra-long sermon, people start looking at their watches. Everyone is thinking the same thing: *"I hope the service goes into overtime!"**

The Church That Peyton Built

I'm sure you picked up on my not-so-subtle point. The above scenario seems beyond crazy to us, but if you take out *church* and put in *football*, then it seems perfectly normal. That scene can be seen as tame at numerous college and professional football stadiums every weekend in the fall and winter. And if you've ever experienced high school football in Texas

A few years ago, my youngest daughter wanted nothing more than to go to an Indianapolis Colts football game. It was the only thing she asked for at Christmas. So her main present that year was a pair of Colts tickets, wrapped up in a Peyton Manning jersey. Since she was only ten at the time, someone needed to take her, and I was willing to make that sacrifice. The truth is, I'm a huge sports fan, and she came by her NFL devotion through me.

It was a Sunday afternoon game, but we drove down on Saturday evening to make sure we would be at the stadium in plenty of time. We woke up early on Sunday and went to a local church. She

---

* Hey, a pastor can dream, can't he?

begged me to let her wear her Peyton Manning jersey to the worship service, but I told her that people wouldn't be wearing Colts gear to church.

I have never been more wrong in my life.

We sat in the back and gazed upon a sea of blue. Thirty-seven people wore Peyton Manning jerseys. She counted. Two people had their faces painted.

A few hours later, I sat among eighty thousand fans in Lucas Oil Stadium, and, yes, I had my own face painted. We both cheered until we lost our voices. We made a great memory and had a blast. But on the drive home, as my exhausted daughter slept, I couldn't help but think about the fact that I had really attended two worship services that day. The question I kept asking myself was, *Which one was I most passionate about?*

It wouldn't be hard to make a case that our culture has turned entertainment into a religion. But let's stay with sports for a moment. Charles S. Prebish, a professor of religious studies at Pennsylvania State University, doesn't believe our passion for it is *like* a religion. He flat-out says sports are "America's newest and fastest-growing religion, far outdistancing whatever is in second place."[13]

Its temples are the great stadiums that are sacred ground to many. Its priests are in the zebra stripes. Its gods wear their names on the back of their jerseys. Its liturgy is fan chants, and its sacrifices are the vast amounts of money that fans pay for tickets and team gear.

But the god of sport isn't the only entertainment deity. How about the world of celebrities and the incredible amount of attention that people devote to showbiz couples and activities?

We have celebrities who are famous for being movie or TV or music stars. Then we have people who are famous simply for being famous. Fans are transfixed by the daily life of Kim Kardashian. Celebrity news publications dominate the magazine aisle, filled with the latest struggles of Lindsey Lohan or Amanda Bynes or some other former child star. Some shows are dedicated to showing pictures or videos of celebrities doing things like going to the grocery store, dining at a restaurant, or taking their dog for a walk. It's not what they're doing that's so compelling; it's who they are.

Gamers

The god of video games is on the ascent. Some of you may be aficionados of MMOs, RPGs, RTSs, or RCGs* who spend several days at a time immersed in virtual worlds defined by computer pixels, your true identities lost in the impersonations of elves or ninja warriors. I shudder to think how many hours I've spent trying to knock down whatever strange shack the Angry Birds are chirping about. Fortunately, I never got into FarmVille.

Some enthusiasts, known as "extreme gamers," spend nearly fifty hours per week in the glare of a monitor, begrudgingly leaving the screen only to visit the bathroom or get another energy drink. Nearly one in ten people between the ages of eight and eighteen could be classified as clinically addicted to video games.[14] Their brains are wired to need more and more of the unique stimulus of the game, releasing enough of the pleasure-inducing dopamine to hook the gamer.

I recently read a study that classified a fifteen-year-old video game addict as displaying "all the characteristics of a heroin addict. You haven't got someone putting a needle in their arm and having a high, but you've got all the telltale collateral damage of a heroin addict: withdrawal from his family, withdrawal from his friends, lies to cover his addiction. He'll do anything."[15]

What about the amount of time we spend on social networks like Facebook and Tumblr? John Piper put it this way: "One of the great uses of Twitter and Facebook will be to prove at the Last Day

---

*Just in case you aren't a gamer, these acronyms stand for: Massive Multiplayer Online, Role-Playing Game, Real-Time Strategy, and Really Cool Game (I made up the last category).

that prayerlessness was not from lack of time."* The Lord God has often lost out when competing with the gods of entertainment for our time and attention.

I'll tell you the moment that convinced me we had a problem. A few years ago, one of my friends traveled to India on a missions trip. After he returned, he was excited to show me pictures and tell me about his journey. My friend had a picture of what was essentially the family room in an Indian home. The centerpiece, what we'd think of as the mantle, featured a carved idol. He pointed out that every seat in the room was carefully arranged so that it faced this idol.

I shook my head sadly at the sight of a family with a false god at the very center of its world. A few hours later, I walked in the front door of my house and had a seat in my recliner. I grabbed the remote, turned on the TV, and kicked back in the chair.

Suddenly it hit me. My eyes scanned the room slowly, and sure enough every seat in our room was carefully positioned to face the fifty-inch flat screen on my mantel.

Don't get me wrong, I'm not anti-entertainment. I'm just wondering if we've gone from watching it to worshiping it.

Maybe you think, *Worshiping? Really? Aren't you getting a little carried away?*

Well, consider that the average American watches more than four-and-a-half hours of television every day. And a recent study showed that most students spend nearly eight hours a day consuming media — watching TV, listening to music, surfing the Web, social networking, or playing video games.[16]

Our own false gods tend to be invisible to us. I can probably see yours, but I'll miss detecting my own. Here's a clue: Discover what the chairs of your heart are aligned around.

What does everything orbit around in your life? What are the locked-in dates on your calendar?

---

*Yep, he tweeted that: twitter.com/johnpiper.

Some students have shrines to football teams — rooms decked out in team colors. Others are dominated by imagery of Justin Bieber or some other teen heartthrob. My point is that we may shake our heads sadly at the family in India, but we should at least consider the possibility that we all have shrines.

And Now the Good News

Okay, I feel the need to push the pause button at this point, because I fear that this may all sound a little legalistic. I'm not trying to construct a tower of rules or say that entertainment is evil. Far from it. Like sex, entertainment is a gift from God — something that can be good until we turn it into a god.

After all, how can you not be entertained by God's creation? How can we avoid the conclusion that he entertained himself by putting together the world, the stars, and the galaxies? How do you think he intends us to respond to a rainbow or a mountain range or a seashore? He didn't just give us a bare, functional place to live. He gave us a planet of wonders.

And what did he expect people to do on that seventh day of rest that he commanded? We can't sleep for twenty-four hours. Entertainment can be a place of rest for our minds and emotions. Why else do people in every human culture have the ability to laugh and be amused?

He is a God of joy, and he wants us to know that joy. He "richly provides us with everything for our enjoyment" (1 Timothy 6:17).

And think of Jesus, who taught through stories and amusing snippets of life. The story of the prodigal son is often considered the greatest short story ever told. His parables were powerful for teaching because they were powerfully entertaining.

What's the problem with entertainment, then?

Solomon, one of the greatest figures of the Old Testament,

found the answer to that question. He pursued entertainment relentlessly, looking for pleasure.

He chased after it as hard as he could. Solomon was the king of Israel, the son of King David. The Old Testament book of Ecclesiastes is basically the journal he kept while he pursued pleasure. In one of his early entries he writes, "I said to myself, 'Come now, I will test you with pleasure to find out what is good'" (Ecclesiastes 2:1).

Solomon has incredible wealth and power, and he spares no expense in trying to entertain himself. He begins with laughter. He tunes into the comedy channel and hires the Jim Gaffigan of his day as a court jester. But he soon concludes that it's meaningless. There's no lasting joy in it.

He tries the life of partying, but sees the emptiness of it quickly. He entertains himself by taking on great projects. He builds houses, plants vineyards, and creates parks. He is a man of many interests, trying to find which, if any, will fill the void in his soul.

He has all the luxuries that vast wealth can afford. He has servants, butlers, maids, chauffeurs, massage therapists, personal shoppers, and even ongoing live entertainment. Ecclesiastes 2:8 tells us that he brought in a choir of men and women — and of course, a harem.

Most people have heard about the harem. The Bible says he had 700 wives and 300 concubines. There are women from every nation, food from every culture, books of wisdom from every civilization. Solomon covers all the bases. He's going to find pleasure if it kills him!

And how does it end? With this exclamation: "Meaningless! Meaningless! Utterly meaningless! Everything is meaningless" (Ecclesiastes 1:2).

Nothing was particularly wrong with his entertainment choices — minus 999 of the women. So what was Solomon's problem? He was trying to make entertainment something it wasn't. He was looking for the meaning of life in amusement.

Spoiler Alert

Solomon gives us a heads up on where pursuing pleasure ultimately leads us. We've seen this bait-and-switch tactic before in the temples of the gods. They offer us the moon and give us a moldy piece of cheese. Sex becomes shame. Entertainment becomes restless boredom.

Have you ever wondered why so many people are bored today? How can anybody get bored during an age of technological wonders and twenty-four-hour streaming videos? Science writer Winifred Gallagher believes boredom is largely a recent problem that is absent from many other cultures. She describes a Western scholar who has lived among the bushmen of Africa for years and become fluent in their language. He has tried over the years to come up with an equivalent to the word *boredom* in their language, but there is a disconnect. They don't understand the concept. The closest they can come to it is *tired*. Our word *boredom* didn't appear in English until the Industrial Age. Yep, that's about the time modern entertainment began to evolve.[17]

And yet the word *amusement* actually comes from the world of worship. Amusement has as its root the word *muse*. The Muses were the female Greek gods who were said to inspire great writing, science, and artistic achievement. They were gods of reflection. When we add the *a* as a prefix, it brings in the idea of "lacking." So amusement is the lack of inspiration, or the lack of reflection.[18]

We seek amusements because we don't want to think. Haven't you ever wandered into the living room after a hard day and just wanted to veg, to watch something mindless? That's fine, up to a point. But don't miss this truth: Instead of inspiring our bored and apathetic existence, the god of entertainment makes us even more that way. Have you ever had a Solomon moment in which you watched your fourth straight "reality show" or flipped through hundreds of channels and concluded "there is nothing on!" What you're really saying is, "Meaningless, meaningless! Utterly meaningless!"

Chasing After the Wind

Solomon pursued entertainment, and here is his conclusion: "I have seen all the things that are done under the sun; all of them are meaningless, a chasing after the wind" (Ecclesiastes 1:14).

Put this book down, go outside, and take three minutes to chase the wind.

Are you back? How'd that go for you? What do you have to show for it?

More than twenty-five years ago, Neil Postman wrote a book called *Amusing Ourselves to Death.* He argued that popular culture is dumbing down our world at a startlingly fast rate. His title captures the power of the god of entertainment. It promises us life, but takes our life from us one thirty-minute sitcom at a time.

Solomon devoted himself to entertainment and concluded it's meaningless.

He wrote his conclusion before the Internet, iPods, and satellite TV. Never in the history of humanity has there been so much entertainment and so little satisfaction.

Solomon does offer a particular, interesting phrase twenty-nine times in Ecclesiastes. It defines the parameters of his search: "under the sun." He has been looking everywhere *under the sun.* He has seen many things *under the sun.* He has found no meaning *under the sun.* No wonder he's tired and frustrated. His sights are set too low; his parameters are too narrow. What he's really searching for is out there, but it isn't *under the sun.*

C. S. Lewis, the great Christian thinker and author of The Chronicles of Narnia, captured it this way: "Creatures are not born with desires unless satisfaction for those desires exists. A baby feels hunger... well, there is such a thing as food. A duckling wants to swim; there is such a thing as water." He goes on to say, "If I find in myself a desire which no experience in this world can satisfy, the most probable explanation is that I was made for another world.

"If none of my earthly pleasures satisfy it, that does not prove the universe is a fraud. Probably earthly pleasures were never meant to satisfy it but only to arouse it, to suggest the real thing."[19]

Ultimately the gods of pleasure can't satisfy our desires. We come to final realization that what we need cannot be found through drugs, through sexuality, or through amusement. We want pure, unadulterated joy, and the trail finally leads to God himself. At the end of Solomon's diary, he reaches this conclusion: "That's the whole story. Here now is my final conclusion: Fear God and obey his commands, for this is everyone's duty" (Ecclesiastes. 12:13, NLT).

We were made for God, and until he is our greatest pleasure, all the other pleasures of this life will lead to emptiness. Augustine expressed this in his prayer nearly fifteen centuries ago: "Our hearts are restless until they find rest in thee."

There is a place in life for relaxation through various forms of entertainment, including sports, television, movies, music, and games, but the question is, Do we seek to fill the spiritual vacuum inside us with empty entertainment, or is it the empty entertainment that is creating the vacuum? I suppose it's the chicken-and-egg question. But there's plenty of evidence that our increasing reliance on the flash and glamour of entertainment is blinding us to quieter and truer pleasures.

Power Off

So how do we smash these idols? How do we kick them off the heart's throne? Often it's as easy as turning off the power.

I'll never forget the first time I went to a church service in Haiti. I had heard from other friends who'd made similar mission trips about worship services lasting four to six hours.

Most preachers in the States would tell you that they start losing people if the church service goes much longer than an hour. There's also the pressure to make sure that hour is filled with enough song-and-dance and multimedia to hold everyone's attention.

So when I got to Haiti, I spoke to the local Haitian pastor about the time differences in our services. I said, "What is it about the Haitian people that keeps them worshiping at church for so many hours?" I was hoping for a profound answer that would redefine my sermons and church services. Here's how he responded. He laughed and said, "In Haiti, we have nothing else to do."

I laughed, but then I was immediately struck by the weight of his answer. They didn't have televisions, radios, phones, computers, theaters. The Lord God didn't have much competition. And then I realized the implications of that.

What if you "went Haitian" for a week or two? What if you had a media fast, other than the requirements of your schoolwork? Can I challenge you to eliminate God's competition, just for a test, and see what happens?

Turn off the TV.

Turn down the music.

Unplug the game console.

Shut down the laptop.

Turn your eyes to the Lord.

Idol ID

What are your favorite forms of entertainment?
Spend some time thinking about your free-time diet. Is it filled with cultural "junk food," or do you watch high-quality movies, read well-written books, listen to uplifting music, and look for intelligent TV broadcasts?

What pop culture icons have been the most influential for you? Given your answers, what insights do your choices offer as to who you really are?

Where and when have you exhibited the most passion and excitement?

People who attend rock concerts tend to show high levels of emotion as various songs are played. Sports fans cry, sing, and even create riots — not just in the United States but across the world, and especially at soccer matches.

Where have you been the most emotionally engaged? How would you compare it to a worship experience?

What kinds of entertainment media have you found to be the most addictive?

Many people are simply hooked on the Internet, spending hour after hour playing games, "Facebooking," or watching videos. Others are addicted to reality TV. Some people can't bear to be without their smartphones or iPods. Entertainment can be as addictive as drugs, alcohol, or anything else.

If you were marooned on a desert island, what forms of entertainment would you miss the most?

Stated another way, which media would you struggle hardest to give up here and now? If there is one you couldn't stand to do without, what does that suggest about its place in your life?

CHOOSING JESUS:

Jesus My Passion

*Idols are defeated not by being removed
but by being replaced.*

The god of entertainment promised us a circus. And in our world filled with obligations and responsibilities, that sounded pretty good.

We looked for amusements to create a sense of wonder. Maybe we would find it in music or in movies or in games or in sports. The god of entertainment was hawking them all, like a carnival barker: "Step right up! Be amazed, be amused! Come one! Come all!"

But in the end, the music was flat, the movies were formulaic, and the games were rigged. The circus left town and we waited impatiently for another one to take its place.

Then we found our passion in Jesus. I get that it may sound ridiculous — how can a dusty old Bible character compete with big-budget movies, action-packed games, or catchy tunes? But once you know Jesus and passionately pursue him, it seems ridiculous that we thought we could ever find what we wanted on a movie screen, a website, or a playlist.

Jesus said in John 10:10, "I have come that they may have life, and have it to the full."

part 3

the temple of power

the god
of appearance

Constance Rhodes didn't have an eating disorder. "I just watch what I eat." Those were the words she repeated to herself and to anyone else who seemed concerned about her weight. *There's nothing wrong with wanting to be thin*, she thought to herself.

Thin people always seemed to be happy and smiling in TV commercials and pictures hanging in stores at the mall. They were the beautiful people. The successful ones. So as a teenager, Constance started replacing that burger and fries with a Diet Coke and fruit plate. Soon she was on a never-ending diet — a dangerous cycle of feast, famine, elation, and self-loathing.

"Even if we are successful at losing a few pounds, it seems we only find new things to dislike about the size and shape of our body," Constance wrote in her book *Life Inside the Thin Cage*.

"If I could be just one size smaller," we lament, *"then everything would be better."*

Constance's mother had battled bulimia when Constance was younger. Her mom was well-educated and understood the dangers of eating disorders. Constance was always bigger than her older sister, but definitely in the "normal" range. Growing up, Constance was content with the way she looked. She enjoyed hanging out with friends, singing in the choir, and overachieving in the classroom. She graduated from high school at sixteen and went straight to college.

That was the same year that a greater concern with her appearance started to take root in her mind. And it didn't take too long before it moved its residency to her heart. Soon her journal entries read:

> Let me tell you about my life inside the thin cage. It is a dark place with little food, little social interaction, and little freedom. Everything is off-limits. Everything is based on performance. If I don't perform well or look good, then I am not good.... Since everything is about performance and appearance, a bad hair day can truly ruin me. If my performance ever slips, I am suddenly in the precarious position of losing my value to the world. Going anywhere and meeting anyone requires that I look my best, for people may not like me if they don't think I'm attractive and thin. I have a hard time sleeping at night. More than anything, I'm alone.[20]

King (or Queen) of the Hill

The god of appearance has no problem finding followers.

He is attractive, compelling, charismatic. He walks into your everyday world and shows you what life could be if you looked just a little bit better. And what he's selling is hard to ignore. He offers us the popularity and envy that makes life sweet.

He plays on the most basic problem of humanity — that pull toward doing it our way, aka pride. *What if your biceps were a little bigger? How would you feel if your thighs were a little bit firmer?*

The gods of appearance are all about personal achievement, rewards we chase and get for ourselves. Is life going to be good? Are we going to be satisfied? The gods of appearance give us very convenient ways to keep score: how we look in the mirror, the size of our clothes, the awards we win, the number of people who know our name.

For many of us, our body becomes our god. It is an object we worship in gym class, perfect in the weight room, and focus on in the cafeteria. We put our hope and find our identity in what the god of appearance offers. And so we diet and we pump iron and we put on makeup and we dress a certain way to make it to the top.

Did you play a game in grade school called King of the Hill? Or maybe you called it King of the Mountain. When I was in the fourth grade, we played that game every day at recess. It went like this: All the boys would push and shove each other to the ground, and when the whistle blew, whoever was left standing on the hill was crowned king.

My guess is that most schools have outlawed such games these days, because of the sheer brutality. I loved this game. You know why? Because I was the undisputed, undefeated king of the hill.*

I was enjoying my reign as king, and then one day we got a new student in our class. This student was bigger and taller than me. Worst of all, this student was a girl.

At first, I didn't sweat it. I thought, *What self-respecting girl would ever want to play King of the Hill?* But I hadn't reckoned on this girl being Barbara.†

Barbara wore cowgirl boots. But I knew I was in real trouble when we were sitting in art class on her second day of school and Barbara ate glue. I'd heard about glue-eaters from other schools, but this was my first real-life encounter.

Sure enough, at recess that day, Barbara wanted to play King of the Hill. In hindsight, it would have been sensible to have a "no girls allowed" rule. I figured it was implied. We were after all playing *King* of the Hill, not Queen of the Hill or Intergender Overlord of the Hill.

I tried politely explaining this to Barbara. But you can hang

---

*Full disclosure: I was the same size in the fourth grade as I am now and was already shaving.

†Hey, Barbara, if you are reading this — I'm talking about a different Barbara.

this on a wall, sew it into a pillow, and post it on Facebook: There is no reasoning with a glue-eater. Barbara dug her boots into the ground and came after me. When the whistle blew that day, I was no longer king. I had been dethroned by a girl. I still remember what a horrible feeling that was. The rest of my fourth grade year, I was consumed with plots to dethrone the evil queen and reclaim my rightful place.

I've discovered that King of the Hill isn't just a childhood game we play, but often ends up becoming our life's pursuit: do whatever it takes to make it to the top. As "king," I was popular, I was known, I was strong. I liked being king.

The gods of appearance and success encourage you to find your worth inside of yourself instead of depending upon Jesus to fill you up. The image staring back at you in a mirror is more important than how much you reflect Christ in your words, actions, and attitudes. Your value in others' eyes is more important than your value in Christ. This is one of the reasons I believe that many of the world's "beautiful" people often have a hard time becoming followers of Christ. Being a devoted disciple means they must acknowledge their own helplessness and their ultimate need — the need for rescue. The god of appearance tells them that they can save themselves.

The Bible addresses our appearance in numerous passages. If you're a young woman, maybe you are familiar with 1 Peter 3:3 – 4 that says, "Your beauty should not come from outward adornment, such as elaborate hairstyles and the wearing of gold jewelry or fine clothes. Rather, it should be that of your inner self, the unfading beauty of a gentle and quiet spirit, which is of great worth in God's sight." I don't want to belabor this point, but it's worth bringing up: There's nothing wrong with wanting to look your best. Having a pleasant appearance isn't a sin. Our bodies are a gift from God and we should take care of them. Dressing thoughtfully, following good hygiene, and careful grooming can draw people to ourselves and ultimately to God. But as we mentioned in an earlier chapter, God cares more about our hearts. The apostle Peter writes these verses as a reminder of that fact.

During this time, some of the Egyptian women spent hours fixing their hair, painting on makeup, and putting together the perfect outfit. (Does that sound familiar?) So Peter is reminding Christ followers that God is more concerned with how your insides are looking than your outside packaging. Sure, you can braid your hair, wear jewelry, and wear nice clothes. But don't let those things consume you. God would rather see you growing closer to him than conforming to the dress size of the latest supermodel.

And while many Scriptures about appearance are aimed at women, guys don't get off the hook.* The Lord knows that the god of appearance often plays to male pride. The apostle Paul wrote a lot about sports and training in the New Testament. And he says this in 1 Timothy 4:8: "For physical training is of some value, but godliness has value for all things, holding promise for both the present life and the life to come."

Look at your life. Do you spend as much time training spiritually as you do building up your physical body? This isn't meant to be a guilt trip. Paul doesn't say physical training is a bad thing. In other places in the Bible, he even encourages us to train in such a way to win the prize. But earthly honors aren't Paul's aim and they shouldn't be ours either. When we focus on being more like God, it benefits us in this life and our life to come in heaven.

For some people, the idea of standing before God without an impressive list of accomplishments is unthinkable. We want to look the part of a good Christian and prove our worth. But to God, success is precisely the opposite of that. It's being willing to step

---

* And if you're a girl who's not into fashion and beauty stuff, just insert yourself when I say "guys / males." It all still applies, and I promise you can shift back into your femalehood right after this section. Same goes for the section above, and any guys who spend a little too much time on their hair in the morning — you know who you are.

away from all the stuff, all the trappings of appearance, and say, "None of that means a thing to me, Lord. I lay it all before you. You and only you are my success."

Behind the Scenes

Where does the god of appearance come from? Like many false gods, it often originates and grows from our own human natures. In Constance's case, and for many people in this entertainment age, Hollywood and advertisers shaped how she viewed herself. The same thing is true for us. How we view ourselves is often a result of the images we let into our minds. And here's a secret: What we see isn't always real.

Okay, it may not be a secret that the images in magazine ads, on billboards, and at department stores are digitally altered. Designers use Photoshop to make supermodels look even more super. While the resulting images may look beautiful, the effects of those photos are downright ugly.

In 2012, Julia Bluhm, a fourteen-year-old in Maine, grew tired of hearing her friends in ballet class complain that they were fat. They weren't. They were beautiful, healthy, athletic dancers. Julia and her friends talked about their feelings and discovered they were comparing themselves to images they saw in magazines. Who could measure up? No one. So Julia decided to do something about it. In March of that year, she started an online petition asking *Seventeen* magazine to stop photoshopping their images and to always include one photo of a regular girl in every issue.

"For the sake of all the struggling girls all over America, who read *Seventeen* and think these fake images are what they should be, I'm stepping up," Julia wrote. "I know how hurtful these photoshopped images can be. I'm a teenage girl, and I don't like what I see. None of us do."

More than 25,000 people signed her online petition in the first two weeks. A couple of months later, Julia and her friends stood in front of the offices for *Seventeen* magazine in New York City holding nearly 85,000 signatures and signs that read, "Teenage Girls Against Photoshop!"

Seventeen magazine heard her complaints and responded. In the August issue, the editor published "*Seventeen* Magazine's Body Peace Treaty." The article promised to do *more* than Julia was asking for. Everybody on the magazine staff signed a pact to "never change girls' body or face shapes" and to "celebrate every kind of beauty in our pages."[21]

But magazines aren't the only place where unattainable images can be found. Hollywood's big screens abound with unrealistic images. No, film editors don't go frame by frame altering the appearance of movie stars. But many actors use cosmetic surgery and performance-enhancing drugs to achieve their Hollywood appearances.

A recent story in *The Hollywood Reporter* details the rise in steroid and HGH use among Hollywood's leading men.

COUNTING THE COST

Years ago on *Saturday Night Live*, Billy Crystal developed a character named Fernando who liked to say, "It is better to look good than to feel good." While the line was said as a joke, a lot of people must feel that way. Just check out how much money is spent to keep up appearances:

- Health clubs rake in about $20 billion a year.
- $20 billion is also the yearly revenue of the U.S. weight-loss industry — including diet books, diet drugs, and weight-loss surgeries.
- $8 billion is spent on cosmetics each year.

> • In 2012, Americans spent $11 billion of cosmetic surgeries, which include Botox injections, face lifts, breast augmentations, and other procedures.*
>
> ---
>
> * statistics from "The Business of Staying Fit," October 11, 2011, http://www. bizologie.com/the-business-of-staying-fit (accessed October 12, 2013); "The Weight-Loss Industry By the Numbers," May 8, 2012, http://abcnews.go.com/ Health/100-million-dieters – 20-billion-weight-loss-industry/story?id=16297197 (accessed October 12, 2013); "Matters of Scale — Spending Priorities," http:// www.worldwatch.org/node/764 (accessed October 12, 2013); Ethan A. Huff, "The United States of Plastic Surgery," May 2, 2013, http://www.naturalnews. com/040164_plastic_surgery_breast_augmentation_botox.html (accessed October 12, 2013).

In the past, Charlie Sheen told *Sports Illustrated* how he took steroids in his younger days to prepare for roles. Mickey Rourke and Arnold Schwarzenegger have also opened up about using performance enhancing drugs. Other actors have maintained their innocence and said they got their six-pack abs the old fashioned way — they earned them.

For instance, elite trainer Mark Twight, who helped Henry Cavill develop his abs of steel for his role as Superman, said that feat was achieved one hundred percent naturally. Twight is known for his natural techniques and difficult workouts — and if you've ever heard other stars, like Hugh Jackman, talk about what they need to do to become superheroes, you know the natural process is far from fun, and LONG. No wonder other stars seem to radically change their body shape in mere months, resorting to the easier (and similar final look) process through drugs or surgery.[22]

Years ago, a Hall of Fame tennis player did an advertising campaign where he said, "Image is Everything."* The god of appearance continues to repeat that message today.

---

* Yet he had a mullet. Go figure.

Keeping Score

What are we talking about when we say appearance? It's one of those words that could have a slightly different meaning for each of us. We tend to attach it to a personal goal or way of presenting ourselves. We often tie our appearance to an amount of success we attain or level of popularity that we experience.

Sociologists tell us that our culture defines success as the prestige that comes from attaining an elevated social status. It's winning the public game of King of the Hill. Your hill might be slightly different than mine, but many people agree about the different ingredients that add up to success.

One of those is the god of materialism that we'll explore in the next chapter. What he offers is far more simple. But there's still plenty of allure there. It's about prestige and clout. It's about recognition. It's about having the right shoes on our feet and the right clothes in the closet.

Appearance shares many of those same characteristics, but also often comes with a false modesty. Your coach walks up to you and says, "Five percent body fat. That's pretty impressive." Or your best friend says, "I wish I had your body." You smile modestly and say, "I've been blessed."

Think about the difference between the words *success* and *blessed*. Success speaks of something that we have done or accomplished. The circumstances of your life can be the same, but the word *blessed* is an indication not that you have done something, but that something has been done for you.

Let me put it this way: Success is when we achieve; blessed is when we receive. If we say "I'm successful," we are giving the glory to ourselves. When we say "I'm blessed," we are giving the glory to God.

Jesus gives an in-depth portrait of what it means to be blessed when he begins the Sermon on the Mount. Beginning in Matthew

5, Jesus gives a rather shocking, counterintuitive profile of the successful, blessed individual.

Who is blessed?

He says those who mourn are blessed, for they receive comfort. He says the meek are blessed, and those who are hungry and thirsty for righteousness. The merciful, the pure in heart, peacemakers, people who are mistreated for doing right — all of these people are blessed. And finally, he says people are blessed when they're insulted, persecuted, and lied about because of their pursuit of Jesus.

This list, this redefinition of success, has an order to it that is very important — especially the first thing Jesus mentions. He begins by saying, "Blessed are the poor in spirit, for theirs is the kingdom of heaven" (Matthew 5:3). Blessed are the poor? I know some of you are thinking, *Yes! I win! I am completely broke!*

But Jesus isn't talking about money here. This isn't a reference to how much you either have or don't have. His words are "poor in spirit." Jesus is describing people who know they don't have it all figured out, people who are humble enough to ask for help.

This world emphasizes putting on being a self-sufficient and self-reliant appearance, acting as if we've got it all figured out. But Jesus redefines a successful life as one that humbly says to God, "I can't do this on my own. I need your help." From the world's perspective, that's the opposite of what successful people do.

Rhodes to Recovery

The god of appearance promises popularity and success, but in the end you only get loneliness and failure. That's how Constance Rhodes felt when she wrote that journal entry. And in the short-term things didn't get better. She battled anorexic behaviors through college, and feelings of not measuring up even after she was married and had built a successful marketing career. She looked so good on the outside that nobody imagined how trapped she felt on the inside.

Her recovery started with a simple prayer: "God, make me willing to be willing." She wasn't ready yet to push the god of appearance off the throne of her life, but she *wanted* to be ready. She followed that up with prayers for God to bring a person into her life who could help her. Several weeks later she met Susi, who listened to her problems and helped Constance see herself as God sees her.

"It's important to know that we don't have to be in an incredible spiritual place to take this first step," Constance wrote in her book. "At the time that I began seeking freedom, I was pretty far from God. I did not pray a lot, and I wasn't going to church regularly. But I knew God knew my heart, and it was my heart that I was asking him to change, which he did."[23]

It always starts with the heart. God knew that from the beginning. And when Constance placed him back on the throne of her heart, she escaped her cage and got what she'd always been looking for.

Idol ID

What goals do you have for your appearance?
Everybody has an idea of how they want to appear to the people around them. Some of us are formal goal setters. Others have more vague ideas about what direction we would like to head. How about you? What would you define as a successful appearance? Where did you come up with your definition? Who set the standards of your appearance?

What drives your desire to look good?
Remember, goals to look your best (and be your best) are not necessarily sinful unless they become idols. You could

have a goal, say, to bench press your body weight, simply because God has given you a passion for fitness and working out. You could have a dream of modeling, running a marathon, becoming class president, or any number of other things.

The real questions are, *What drives your goals? What is your motivation? Is it for your glory or God's?*

How often do you find yourself envying beautiful people?

Our culture spends a great deal of time spotlighting those who have made it to the top, based on the world's standards of beauty and success. Do you find yourself filled with envy? Sometimes envy is a leading indicator which god is motivating us. If we feel driven toward certain goals, we may become frustrated when others reach them first. How do you respond when others succeed?

CHOOSING JESUS:

Jesus My Reflection

Idols are defeated not by being removed
but by being replaced.

The god of appearance whispered to us, "Don't you want to be king of the hill?"

"Which hill?" we asked.

"Any of them. All of them." He smiled.

And we pursued a life of climbing, always climbing. Toward popularity. Toward smaller clothing sizes. Toward abs of steel. This god never had to make his case for what he was offering. We could see it every day in advertisements on TV and in magazines.

But along the way, climbing, earning, and achieving became ends in themselves. It was no longer about how we looked, but about whom we looked better than.

If we were honest, we would have to say that we worked harder for an image in the mirror than to reflect God's image.

And we had several unhappy surprises. One was that we were always weary from the effort. We also didn't expect to feel trapped instead of freed. But the greatest surprise was that the top of the hill ended up being a pretty lonely and disappointing place. We wondered if maybe we had the wrong hill.

And then we discovered one last hill. But this hill already had a King, along with three crosses standing on it. And he extends us a simple invitation: "Know the truth, and the truth will set you free." As we follow him, he turns how we look at ourselves on its head.

We find where the Spirit of the Lord is, there is freedom. And we discover the truth of Paul's words in 2 Corinthians 3:18 (HCSB), "We all, with unveiled faces, are looking as in a mirror at the glory of the Lord and are being transformed into the same image from glory to glory."

And so now, we still care about our appearance, but we define it very differently. God has become our standard. We live to be transformed more into his image. That's how we define true beauty.

the god
of materialism

Matthew stared out the window as the bus rolled out of Simón Bolívar International Airport in Caracas, Venezuela. He'd rarely left his home state of Colorado, let alone the country. The sights and sounds of a foreign land at sunset overwhelmed his senses.

His youth pastor had prepared Matthew in many ways for his first missions trip. Matthew had memorized his part in the mimed skit that demonstrated the sacrifice God's Son made for all people. He'd learned how to juggle, so he could help his youth group draw a crowd on the busy streets of Caracas. He'd even written down his personal testimony to share about the change God had made in his life since he'd believed in Jesus as his Savior. But nothing could prepare Matthew for what his guide was about to say.

"Caracas is a city of contrasts," the guide said. "It's a modern city with numerous skyscrapers. Our downtown has many wealthy people with well-paying jobs."

"What are those lights on the hills?" a girl named Becca interrupted, pointing to neighborhoods on the outlying hills where houses seemed to stack on top of each other like LEGOs.

"Those are our *barrios*," the guide replied. "The slums where the poorest of the poor live. You don't want to go there, especially at night."

"Why?" she asked.

"It's too dangerous. Even the police don't go there at night."

Then the guide looked straight at Matthew. "And you would never wear your Nikes in there. Because they'd kill you for your shoes."

Matthew looked down at his new high-tops and shuddered. *My life for a pair of shoes*, he thought. *No way.*

But I've heard similar stories that happened in the United States. In 2012 a man was shot leaving a Houston mall, just for the Nikes he'd purchased in a store. I've also read reports on how families in the inner city will spend hundreds of dollars for shoes or brand-name clothes when they can't even pay their electric bill or buy food.

It may sound crazy to be willing to kill or go hungry for a pair of shoes, but in many ways we all do exactly that by worshiping the god of materialism.

The Almighty Dollar

The god of materialism has been around a long time. Back in the day, you knew him as gold or silver, purple robes, heads of cattle, or animal skins. Before the health of the almighty dollar took a turn for the worse, the god of materialism had come into his own. He was riding high in the modern world as families scrambled to buy a bigger house, the newest SUV, the latest LED TV, or the coolest gadgets. He's always been a god, but he hadn't always enjoyed this kind of power.

In the old days, you see, he was just your garden variety false god. Money was important, but the king had most of it. He owned the palace that was surrounded by teeming hordes of common people who had no wealth and no hope of ever getting any. They caught their fish or plowed their half acre or fought in the army. Rarely did they have two pennies to spend on anything, so they pursued more attainable gods.

Then the world began to change. Democracy created a somewhat more level playing field in the Western world. The god of materialism was the star of the American dream — a house, a white picket fence, a car in the driveway, and a TV in every room. When people talked about their "pursuit of happiness," this god would think to himself, *What they really mean is the pursuit of me.*

Now before we go any further, I think it's important to differentiate between the god of money and the god of materialism. Obviously, they're related. Greed plays a big part in the power these gods hold over us. But the god of money is all about wealth, *just one dollar more.* The god of materialism entices us with what money can buy. It's about status and possessions and pretty things and fun toys. The god of money may be your parents' god. The god of materialism battles for his place in our hearts at a much younger age.

In Luke 12, Jesus is teaching a crowd of thousands. They are captivated as Jesus challenges them to be faithful to God. "If you disown me here on earth," Jesus says, "I will disown you before my Father in heaven." Jesus urges them to see this life through the lens of eternity. But there is a man in the crowd who isn't thinking about heaven. He's got money on his mind. Luke 12:13 reads, "Someone in the crowd said to him, 'Teacher, tell my brother to divide the inheritance with me.'"

It's likely that a younger brother was asking this question. Perhaps he was bothered over the fact that according to the Levitical law, family inheritances gave two-thirds of the possessions to the older son and only one-third to the younger son. Notice that he doesn't really ask Jesus a question about money. He comes to Jesus wanting him to reinforce what he already believes to be true about money and possessions. Sound familiar?

Jesus replied, "Man, who appointed me a judge or an arbiter between you?" Then he turned his attention back to the crowd and added, "Watch out! Be on your guard against all kinds of greed; life does not consist in an abundance of possessions" (Luke 12:14 – 15). Then God's Son goes on to tell a story about a man who made possessions his god. Of the thirty-eight parables Jesus tells, sixteen deal with the subject of money. Jesus seems to make it clear that the god of materialism is often God's main competition for our hearts.

Here's how Jesus told the story in Luke 12:16 – 19: "The ground of a certain rich man yielded an abundant harvest. He thought to himself, 'What shall I do? I have no place to store my crops.'"

So this rich fool (that's probably how the story is labeled in your Bible) has way more than he needs. Then he has a better-than-expected year. So what's this poor chap to do? Jesus tells us: "This is what I'll do. I will tear down my barns and build bigger ones, and there I will store my surplus grain. And I'll say to myself, 'You have plenty of grain laid up for many years. Take life easy; eat, drink and be merry.'"

Mine

This story perfectly describes someone who is worshiping the god of materialism. If you look closely, you'll notice that the man refers to himself nine times in two verses. He speaks of *my* crops, *my* barns, *my* grain. But who gave him the good crops? Who gave him the ability to get rich? It doesn't seem to occur to him that he has what he has because God has given it to him. This guy almost sounds as bad as the seagulls in *Finding Nemo* who fight over everything, saying, "Mine. Mine. Mine. Mine."

When we approach our possessions from the perspective that they belong to us, it just doesn't work. The key to keeping materialism in its right place is to remember that everything belongs to God. Whatever we have is on loan from our heavenly Father. Solomon reminds us in Ecclesiastes 5:15, "Everyone comes naked from their mother's womb, and as everyone comes, so they depart. They take nothing from their toil that they can carry in their hands." Psalm 24:1 simply puts it this way: "The earth is the Lord's, and everything in it." When we keep that perspective, we understand our dependence on God and we worship him as the provider.

Imagine your family makes big plans for spring break. Then your parents' car breaks down and all of the vacation money has to be spent on fixing the engine. Instead of having a blast at the beach, you're staring at a "stay-cation." But one day your parents get an email from an uncle who happens to have a beach house. He says you're welcome to stay in his beach house for a week. He even sends the key and says to make yourself feel at home. Now let's imagine you get to the beach house, walk in, and turn on the light. Nothing happens, because the light bulb is burned out. You look out the window and can barely see the ocean. And to top it off, the pillow on your bed is lumpy. It's all too much to handle, so you fire off an angry text to your uncle laying out everything that is wrong and demanding to know what he is going to do to make it right.

In real life, you would never respond that way. For the entire week at the beach house, you'd be constantly reminded about and grateful for your uncle's generosity.

God has given us the use of his resources here on earth. If we stop and think about it, we have much to be grateful for. Go through your day sometime recognizing that everything is God's. Get out of God's bed, walk into God's bathroom, and turn on God's shower. Then put on God's jeans and zip up God's hoodie. Eat God's cereal.* Drink God's orange juice. Get in God's car and head to school.

When we start to see every possession as God's, it helps us develop an attitude of gratitude that leads to a heart of worship. And when our hearts are focused on worship, there's no room for the god of materialism.

---

*Frosted Flakes.

Divine Attributes of Money

Money isn't the problem. Money is amoral. It's not good or bad in and of itself. But the *love* of money is the root of all kinds of evil. Money and physical wealth holds great potential to become a God substitute for us. When Jesus spoke on idolatry in the Sermon on the Mount, his only application was in the area of money. Matthew 6:24 reads, "No one can serve two masters. Either you will hate the one and love the other, or you will be devoted to the one and despise the other. You cannot serve both God and money." Like the rich fool in Luke 12, we can all too easily attach divine attributes to money and possessions. We look to money to do for us the very thing God wants to do for us. The man in Jesus' story does this as well.

First, he looks to money as his source of security. When we make material things a security blanket, they become our god, because that's where we are putting our hope and our dependence. Prayer becomes a nice idea, but not necessary because we can already meet our own needs.

The gods of power work from one shared premise: we can take care of ourselves. We can find a way to handle all our needs. The Lord is nice, but he's not really necessary. The gods of success appeal to our desire to be self-sufficient.

Second, the man in Jesus' story looks to money as his source of satisfaction. He thinks to himself, *If I just accumulate a little more, I can take life easy.* His possessions make him happy. And you have to wonder: If things continued to go his way, would his new barns be big enough? Or would his happiness depend on getting bigger barns later? This mindset isn't unique. You have a decent car (well, at least it runs and gets you where you need to go) and an afterschool job that pays for gas and leaves you enough extra cash for some fun as well as some savings, and life is pretty good, all things considered. But you look at the lifestyles of the rich and famous and say, "If I just had a sports car and vaults of money, then I'd be truly happy."

And that might be true to a point. A 2006 study found that someone making $20,000 per year will indeed be happier than someone at poverty level. After all, he isn't worried about his next meal or whether he'll continue to have shelter. But more money doesn't determine a person's level of happiness. Surprisingly, someone who makes $100,000 annually isn't much happier than the employee making $20,000. Huge difference in salary, but a minimal difference in happiness. As a matter of fact, the wealthier people are, the less time they spend pursuing enjoyable activities. The researchers concluded that "the belief that high income is associated with good mood is wide-spread but mostly illusory."[24] Ecclesiastes 5:10 says, "If you love money, you will never be satisfied; if you long to be rich, you will never get all you want" (GNT).

Last, this man from Jesus' story looks to money as his *source of significance*. His focus is on himself and how much he has accumulated. He clearly found his identity in his stuff. We often do the same thing. We judge our worth by what we're wearing, our collection of video games, or the money we have saved for college.

THE COST OF A SMILE

Psychologists have studied what makes people happy. Not only do many of them find that money can't buy it; the opposite seems to hold true in many cases.

"Materialism is toxic for happiness," says University of Illinois psychologist Ed Diener. His research indicates that those who are less concerned about accumulating and spending are more likely to experience contentment.

University of Michigan psychologist Christopher Peterson

---

indicates that forgiveness is the trait most strongly linked to happiness. Peterson has said, "It's the queen of all virtues, and probably the hardest to come by."*

* Marilyn Elias, "Psychologists Now Know What Makes People Happy," *USA Today*, December 10, 2002, www.usatoday.com/news/health/2002–12–08-happy-main_ x.htm (accessed October 21, 2013).

The god of materialism wants us to believe that our significance comes from what we have. But we find our true identity in Christ. He has marked us as his own, and that's what makes us valuable. He forever determined our value when he died on the cross for us. But when we worship the god of materialism, a person's worth is determined not by the symbol of the cross, but by the symbol of a dollar sign.

The man in Luke 12 had put his trust in his money and possessions. His plan was to retire early and eat, drink, and be merry. But that's not what happened. Luke 12:20 records the end of the story: "But God said to him, 'You fool! This very night your life will be demanded from you. Then who will get what you have prepared for yourself?'" The man died that very night, and everything he'd accumulated bought him nothing but a nicer funeral.

Is it possible that you have ascribed to money some of these divine attributes? Are you looking to possessions to do for you what God wants to do for you? Currency in the United States has a slogan stamped right on its face that reads, "In God We Trust." That's more than a little ironic given the fact that so many of us have put our trust in money as god. It might be more accurate to put a question mark at the end of that statement, so it would read, "In God We Trust?" How we view our possessions has a way of answering that question.

Most all of us have an appetite for money or possessions. We think that if we could satisfy this appetite it would go away — if we could just make the money or buy the latest tablet — but that's not how it works. Instead, the more you feed it, the hungrier it gets.

Jesus put it this way in Matthew 6:21: "Where your treasure is, there your heart will be also." Where we put our money reveals what we've put our trust in.

Idol ID

How often do you compare what you have to other people?
The world teaches us to measure one another by labels on our jeans or the icons on our smartphone. The better they are or the more we have, the more important we are. Whether we truly, practically need more things or not, we chase after them for the affirmation they give us.

Are you content with your possessions? Or do you have iPhone envy? If so, it might indicate that materialism is becoming a god in your life.

How much anxiety do material possessions add to your life?
If you were to rank the things that cause you the greatest stress, where would your possessions be on that scale? Do you easily let your little sister borrow your clothes or loan out a video game to a friend, or do you hold your things tightly and worry that someone might ruin them?

There are many examples in the Bible about people being more important than possessions. The apostle Paul wrote specifically about giving thanks in *all* circumstances and being content in any and every situation, whether he was well fed or hungry. Can you give thanks and be content with what you have?

To what extent are your dreams and goals driven by things?

We've talked about personal dreams in this book, because they tell us a great deal about who we are and what makes us tick. What is your greatest dream, the thing that comes to your mind the quickest when someone asks, "If you had one wish?"

Do your dreams involve wealth and luxury? Winning the lottery? If so, why?

Be honest with yourself as you reflect upon why you want to pursue a certain career when you're older. Would you want to be a doctor to help people or because you would make a lot of money?

What is your attitude toward giving?

Think about occasions when you've been given a big check for your birthday or just been paid for babysitting or received a paycheck at your part-time job. Is that money already spent in your mind? Do you know where every dollar is going — and none of them are going to the church? What percentage of your money do you currently give away? Deuteronomy 14:23 reads, "The purpose of tithing [giving ten percent] is to teach you to always put God first in your life" (LB). Do you look at money as only a way to purchase things? Or do you find enjoyment and inspiration in using your finances to help others? Are you willing to loan twenty dollars to a friend who needs help without expecting to be paid back? Or could that twenty dollars ruin your friendship if it's not returned as soon as possible?

CHOOSING JESUS:

Jesus My Provider

*Idols are defeated not by being removed
but by being replaced.*

The god of materialism was almost irresistible. He spun tales of high-speed computers, luxurious clothes, cool cars, and all the good things we could have. Yes, we had heard the old refrain that money can't buy happiness. We knew that. We had seen what it had done to other people over and over.

But we were going to be different. We would know how to handle our possessions without letting them rule us. We didn't want to buy happiness, we just wanted to rent a little pleasure. But somewhere it all went wrong. Somehow the god of materialism became a slave driver.

He kept us following him, trying to keep him from getting away. We thought our things would provide us with security, significance, and some measure of satisfaction. But strangely, even when we filled our lives with things, we still felt empty inside.

Then we chose Jesus and discovered that he is our provider. He provides everything we need. He provides us with security because he never leaves us or forsakes us. He provides us with significance because our identity and value are found in his love. He provides us with satisfaction because our souls were made for him. We discovered that God would meet all our needs according to the riches of his glory in Christ Jesus.

the god
of achievement

Taylor Hooton dreamed of pitching on the varsity baseball team at Plano West Senior High School. As a junior, he'd recorded a save at the varsity level. Now his focus was on making the leap to full-time varsity starter for his senior season.

At six feet and one-and-a-half inches, Taylor had a big frame. And he'd grown from 175 pounds to 205 pounds during the winter and spring, thanks to hard work in the weight room. At least, that's what his parents thought.

Sure, Taylor was hitting the weights. But he'd also started using injectable and oral steroids as a little extra boost. The drugs worked. They made him bigger and stronger. They also caused him to develop acne on his back and made him irritable, aggressive, and prone to fits of rage.

His family noticed his change in behavior, even more than they noticed the change in his body. Taylor had always been well-liked at school and popular with girls. He had friends in all different social circles. He was known for his smile and respectful attitude. But now he was grouchy, stole from his parents, and pushed people away.

And the really sad thing is Taylor didn't need the steroids to be a star athlete. Baseball ran in his blood. His brother pitched in college. His cousin, Burt Hooton, had pitched in the major leagues. He had all the skills and all the natural ability he needed to achieve his dreams. [25]

But the god of achievement is always whispering in your ear: *You have to do more. You're not good enough on your own. You're nothing without me.*

Merit Badges

There is something within us that loves to *git-r-done.*

Comedian Larry the Cable Guy has made millions because we can all relate to that catchphrase. In the Western world, it's simply part of our DNA to make something happen on our own. Many of the first settlers of North America were very devout Christians who believed that God honors hard work and determined effort. The United States of America has been an experiment in freedom, an exercise in liberating people to go as far as their work will take them.

The problem is we're all in danger of exchanging one king for another. If you've read this far, you'd probably agree that we're built to bow. We must find someone or something to serve. It's not surprising that, in our culture, personal achievement is a very powerful and alluring idol.

Think about our experience as children: Cub Scouts to Boy Scouts, Brownies to Girl Scouts. These are wonderful organizations, by the way, that teach any number of positive values — in particular, the value of achievement. You perform a task, and you win a merit badge. Go on a hike and fulfill the given requirements, and you receive that colorful "camping" patch. Do you remember how great it feels when the scoutmaster pins that patch to your uniform?

That's the same feeling we get when we add pins or patches to a letterman jacket. Or maybe you're a high-achiever type who finds their identity in good grades and making the honor roll and earning a spot with National Honor Society. Others love the spotlight of landing the lead role in the musical or getting the solo in the choir. And many of us have long-term goals of what we could achieve by making it into the right college and building the right career. Who knows what we could achieve one day?

And so the vest wrapped with badges, the jacket covered in patches, the trophies on the shelf, the ribbons, the medals, the report cards, the diplomas, and one day the degrees, the promotions, the paychecks can become idols that we bow down to. They represent what we have accomplished through our hard work and dedication.

Obviously there is nothing wrong with any of these achievements. In fact, these achievements can be acts of worship that glorify God. But when our lives are all about getting things done, we can find that there is not much room for God. Instead, our approach to worshiping God can turn into checking off a box on our to-do list labeled "Go to church."

Making the Choice

In Luke 10, Jesus only has about six months left on earth, and he knows what's coming. He spoke about the road to Jerusalem and what would soon happen. Jesus was certainly a high achiever. He needed only a few years of ministry and a dozen guys to turn the world upside down.

But Jesus wasn't preoccupied with a checklist of things to do and objectives to meet every day. He simply did whatever the Father wanted him to do and ended up achieving more than anyone in history. He regularly took time to get away and pray.

Even though he has lots to do and only a little time on this particular day, Jesus took time to stop and visit with a few good friends, Mary and Martha. They're the two sisters of Lazarus, and Jesus clearly has a special relationship with the family. The Scriptures tell us that Martha opened her home to Jesus, and the following scene took place: two sisters, one hurrying around frantically making the home worthy of Jesus, the other sitting quietly at his feet, listening.

> But Martha was distracted by all the preparations that had to be made. She came to him and asked, "Lord, don't you care that my sister has left me to do the work by myself? Tell her to help me!"
>
> "Martha, Martha," the Lord answered, "you are worried and upset about many things, but few things are needed — or indeed only one. Mary has chosen what is better, and it will not be taken away from her."
>
> — Luke 10:40–42

A lot of things are going on in those five sentences, but if we look at this story through the lens of idolatry, there are two significant phrases:

- Martha was distracted.
- Mary had chosen.

The god of achievement distracts us from following Jesus by reminding us of all the things that need to be done. How often do we live with good intentions of spending time with Jesus and turning our heart toward him only to find at the end of the day that's the one thing on our checklist that we never got around to?

There are a few reasons why the god of achievement so often wins the daily battle for our hearts. He offers a method of measurement. For many of us, it's much easier to give our time to what is tangible. We like to see what we get done. For instance, in my life I can see when the house is cleaned, or the grass mowed, or the book got finished, or the groceries bought. When I get through spending time with Jesus, I don't see immediate results. When I paint a room, the change is obvious. When I spend time in prayer and worship, it lacks visual evidence that I've accomplished anything.

Mary was distracted by the preparations. She had a to-do list that needed to be done right now. Notice that what Mary was doing wasn't evil or sinful. In fact what she was doing was good, because she was doing it for Jesus. But Jesus says Mary had chosen better. What we are doing may be good, but the good is bad when there is something better.

Once again we see that many of the gods that battle for our hearts don't try to lure us with what is obviously wrong or overtly sinful. The issue of idolatry comes down to one word: choice. We've heard it from Moses. We've heard it from Joshua. We've heard it from Elijah. Now we hear it from Jesus. He commends Mary for the choice that she made.

A Little Competition

Martha demonstrates another characteristic of someone who struggles with the god of achievement. She compares herself and seems to be keeping score. Martha makes a point of how much more she has done than Mary. High achievers will turn almost anything into a competition. There are two related symptoms that indicate that the god of achievement has gained some ground in your life:

1. A constant frustration with people in your life who, from your perspective, aren't getting it done. Martha is frustrated that Mary isn't being a better teammate, but Mary doesn't even realize she's competing in a game. This frustration with others for not doing their fair share comes to the surface in the form of criticism. Martha is critical of Mary's lack of productivity. Are you constantly critical of those around you for not getting enough done or not doing it well enough?

2. The second symptom is a constant sense of discontentment with yourself for not getting done what you hoped you would. Thomas J. DeLong, a Harvard Business School

professor, interviewed five hundred "high-need-for-achievement professionals." More than four hundred of them "questioned their own success and brought up the name of at least one other peer who they felt had been more successful than they were."[26] What's interesting is that these professionals were some of America's top corporate leaders, yet they were making themselves miserable by constantly comparing themselves to others. Maybe you do the same thing with a classmate, friend, or sibling?

When we worship the god of achievement, getting things done and getting them done right becomes more important than anything or anyone. In Psalm 46:10, the Lord reminds us to "be still, and know that I am God." It's hard to worship the god of achievement and be still and worship the Lord God at the same time. When you can't be still to connect with Christ because you always have to be doing, that should be a warning sign. The rest of that verse in Psalm 46 goes on to say, "I will be exalted among the nations, I will be exalted in the earth."

When we slow down long enough to know that the Lord is God, we are reminded of his sovereignty. He's got the whole world in his hands. Can I encourage you next time you find yourself being critical of others or especially hard on yourself to remember Mary and choose what is better?

Choosing Better

Most of us resonate with Martha because we are an achievement-based culture. This is the ADD generation.* We're always on the move, always trying to get something done. Our phones are constantly dinging to let us know there is a text we need to return, a post we need to make, or something important we're going to be late for.

---

*Squirrel.

Martha had Jesus in her presence, and she was cooking and cleaning. Just imagine what would've happened if her grandchildren one day asked her, "What was it like? Jesus in your home! That must have been amazing. What did he say?"

And she'd have to tell them, "Well, to tell the truth, there was this special china I was trying to find. It had been in our family for a long time, and I just had to have that for dinner with Jesus. So I never really heard what he said. I just caught bits and pieces of the conversation as I flew through the room. Your great-aunt Mary will have to fill you in."

How many times have we been so distracted that we've missed a divine moment? How many things does God long to say to us, but he keeps getting our voicemail because we're too busy to pick up? It's idolatry of a dangerous sort, because it appears to be based on virtue and traditional values — and all those "apply yourself" talks your parents might be fond of giving. Work hard. Don't be like that loafer, Mary! Who's going to get this stuff done?

I wonder how important that stuff was to Martha after her friend had been crucified, resurrected, and taken up into heaven. I wonder what she would have given for just a few moments to sit at his feet.

"Mary has chosen what is better."

That's a choice we can make every single day when we choose to make our relationship with God more important than anything else on our to-do list. I know I've already said this, but I want to be clear: Working hard and achieving goals are an important part of leading a God-glorifying life. But they are not life. They are not even a measuring stick for the worth of life.

When we give our achievements our soul, they become one more false god — a great cluster of merit badges, melted into a golden calf. Remember, the people had asked for "gods who will go before us" (Exodus 32:1). That's what we want our achievements to do — to pave the way as we move through life.

And when Aaron helped make the idol, the people said, "These are your gods, Israel, who brought you up out of Egypt" (Exodus 32:4). It seems crazy. How could they make something, then give it credit for where they had come?

That's the illusion of achievement. What we've done begins to define who we are. We are our achievements. We're the star football player or the head cheerleader, the captain of the chess club, the president of National Honor Society, the future ivy league student, the lead in the school play. When God is on the throne of our hearts, we're all of that — but none of it matters. All that truly defines us is being God's child.

We all need to take a deep breath. Be still. And know the Lord is God.

Stock Options

Chuck Colson is one of the most famous Christians to live in the last fifty years. He rose to political power at a young age, became disgraced, and was imprisoned after the Watergate scandal in the 1970s. (If you haven't heard about him in a history class yet, you probably will hear him mentioned at some point.) Chuck gave his life to Christ in 1973 and continued to be a high achiever. He founded Prison Fellowship, a ministry where countless thousands of prisoners have found Jesus and turned their lives around. Chuck wrote numerous bestselling books, hosted a popular radio commentary, and became one of the most influential men in America.

He understood that life is made of choices. He admitted that he'd made his fair share of mistakes. And he didn't want young people to make the same ones he did, so he would advise students, "Just stop occasionally. Take stock of who you are and what you're doing. I never did that. I was too busy."

From the distance of years, Chuck realized he had gone so far and enjoyed it too little. Who had time to enjoy? The work was sacred.

Achievements are good things until they become our gods. They can help make this world a better place. But in the end, we can't put our faith in them because they shrivel like all the stuff of the world. That's why Paul wrote in 2 Corinthians 4:18, "So we fix our eyes not on what is seen, but on what is unseen, since what is seen is temporary, but what is unseen is eternal."

A few years ago, a group of senior citizens, all at least ninety-five years old, were asked this question: "If you had life to live all over again, what would you do differently?"

They weren't given multiple-choice answers but allowed to say whatever they were thinking. The responses varied, of course, but three themes dominated their replies:

1. If I had life to live all over again, I would reflect more.
2. If I had life to live all over again, I would risk more.
3. If I had life to live all over again, I would do more things that would live on after I am dead.[27]

I believe there's deep wisdom to be gained from the observations of this world's experienced sojourners. What they're saying to us here is, I wish I had slowed down a little. I wish I hadn't always played it safe, but had really gone for it occasionally. And I wish I had invested myself not in these rusty merit badges, but in eternal realities.

A Tragic Ending

Taylor's dreams were in reach, but then his life started to spin out of control. The steroids turned him into a person he didn't recognize. Gone was the fun-loving athlete with lots of friends. Now anger ruled his life.

Once he got so mad that he punched the floor and injured the knuckles on his pitching hand.

The god of achievement promises accolades and honors, but

then strips even those away. The home – run-hitting baseball player gets banned due to using performance-enhancing drugs. The workaholic burns out and loses his job and his identity.

Taylor finally admitted his steroid use to his brother. But eventually, his parents became suspicious and demanded that he be tested. The test came back clean.

Heading into the summer of his senior year, Taylor tried to get off the steroids. But losing the euphoria and aggression he felt while taking the drug led him into depression. He saw a counselor. Nothing seemed to help. He felt trapped.

Then in July, he got in an argument with his parents about being grounded. They wanted him to change his habits and stop stealing from the family. He couldn't handle the punishment. He went to his room and hung himself.[28]

His death shocked his school and the nation. Taylor had everything going for him. He was attractive, athletic, well-liked, and smart. Now he was gone. His father, Don, started the Taylor Hooton Foundation to educate other students about the dangers of performance-enhancing drugs. No dream is worth your life. No achievement is worth risking your health.

Yet statistics show that 1.5 million students — about 6 percent of high school and middle school students — use anabolic steroids. Some use because coaches tell them they're too small and need to get bigger to make the team. But about half of the students aren't even athletes. They take these drugs to improve their appearance and achieve their goals of beauty or success.[29]

If you're an achievement addict, consider this your wake-up call. Stop to reflect, to think about who you are and who you will be when all the earthly accomplishments have dried up and blown away. Consider the words of Jesus to Martha, the hard-learned lesson from Taylor Hooton's life, and the wise words from Chuck Colson. And don't just choose what is good — choose what is better.

Idol ID

How has your life up to now been defined by achievement?
How much do your parents, coaches, and teachers ingrain in you that you need to be highly productive, whether in schoolwork or other activities? In what area do you want to achieve greatness?

Once again, achievement is good, but sometimes we get the idea that what we achieve is who we are, or that it determines our value and justifies our existence.

How do you define your identity to others? To yourself?
Most of us begin with our name and proceed to our activities when introducing ourselves to others. It makes sense: We're identifying how we spend a great amount of our time and what our important skills are. But to what extent do we consider our achievements as defining us? Are you your spot on the varsity team? Is performing the great driving force in your life?

Why do you do what you do?
Think through what you're currently working hard to achieve. Hard work is good but why are you doing it? Is it to prove yourself? Is it because of your competitive drive to be the best? Or are you working hard for the glory of God?

When do you feel the most guilty or self-critical?
Does a lack of productivity — even for a mere day or a couple of hours — bring you frustration and cause you to feel bad about yourself?

CHOOSING JESUS:

Jesus My Goal

Idols are defeated not by being removed
but by being replaced.

The god of achievement called out to us with illusions of grandeur. Getting the lead in the musical. Hitting the game-winning shot. Becoming class president. Being accepted into the right college. He promised satisfaction, fame, and popularity. He drove us to work harder, volunteer more, build a better résumé.

Instead of a human *being*, we became a human *doing*. We didn't have time to enjoy our friends, our family, God's creation. We went from one obligation to the other, running ourselves ragged for this false god.

We thought our achievements would bring us happiness and significance. But every time we met one goal, another seemed just out of reach. We constantly strained to do more, be more, achieve more.

Then we chose Jesus and discovered that he is our goal. He doesn't look at our ability to accomplish things for him. He's more concerned about our availability to follow him. Instead of a to-do list, Jesus tells us to "Come to me...for my yoke is easy and my burden is light" (Matthew 11:28, 30).

We learned to feel the freedom of being in the will of God, where we can experience the whole process of achieving and not simply the results. We became less competitive with others, and gave ourselves the permission to fail. Ironically, in the end this freedom to fail often allowed us to achieve greater results.

And so now we understand that work and achievements

are blessed by God. Even Adam and Eve received work assignments in the garden. But now we aren't driven by achievement. Our feelings of joy are no longer linked to achievements, but to serving and becoming more like God.

part 4

the temple of love

the god
of romance

Remember the elementary school playground? When all the boys got together to play some ball, one of the guys was often, well, a gal. It's a classic playground tradition for a "tomboy" to get into the middle of athletic competition. Of course, everyone usually figures the tomboy will grow up into the traditional "girl next door."

Shannon showed no signs of moving in that direction. A tomboy since childhood, she continued to push the masculine side of her personality to the forefront. She came to think of herself as a living, walking mistake. When God made her, she figured, he'd poured a boy spirit into a girl body.

There were reasons. Shannon had been a victim of sexual abuse. That experience damages people in different ways. For Shannon, it was an indication that being a girl placed her in danger — being pretty or feminine made her a target. Things were done to girls. If she wasn't a girl, maybe they'd leave her alone.

Shannon also came out of her abuse with a distorted view of relationships with the opposite sex. Though she hung out with guys and participated in sports with them, she had no clue how to relate to them outside of athletics.

Most of all, she believed that she had no real value as a human being. Otherwise, why would anyone have done that to her? The abuser was a male authority figure who she was supposed to be able to trust. So who or what in life could be counted on? The question seemed rhetorical, because there was no apparent answer.

Shannon's only response was to toughen up. She wore her hair short, focused on sports, and stayed grimy and sweaty as much as possible. It matched the dirtiness she felt on the inside. She was sarcastic and assertive, but it was only a mask to hide the depression and confusion beneath the surface.

All of this was relatively manageable until she hit puberty. Before that, Shannon could simply be a little girl climbing trees, stealing second, playing catch. But as adolescence approached, things started to change. The girls painted their nails and talked about clothing. She didn't fit into that world at all. And the dynamic changed with guys too. It wasn't cool to be a tomboy anymore, as boys began to relate to girls through attraction rather than athleticism.

Shannon had no place at all. *I'm a mistake, a misfit*, she thought. *I have no future.*

As she thought about it, she realized that she craved love — to give it and to receive it. Love could rescue her from shame. It could make her feel like a person of worth. Like many, she sexualized the feelings in her heart. So desperate was her desire for caring that she reached back to the time of her abuse and took hold of the idea of sexual expression she found there. It was the most obvious way to get attention, to find some form of love.

It was unhealthy. It was self-destructive. But it was all she knew. She understood the deal. I will consent to this, let you do that, and you will give me love and acceptance in return. But, of course, no real connections came out of that arrangement. She offered sex, and that's all she got back. Throwing herself at boys didn't make her feel any more complete as a girl. She coveted love and acceptance from her own gender. Almost inevitably, she began to wonder about a lesbian identity. She pursued the question not overtly, but through pornography.

Again, she was exploring the question of love through sexualizing it. This hadn't helped her understand boys, and it didn't help her understand girls. Once again her pursuit of love didn't bring her any sense of acceptance or belonging. In fact, the harder she chased it, the lonelier she felt. She tried desperately to satisfy the hunger in her heart for intimacy, but instead she felt a growing sense of isolation.

The Myth of Hearts, Flowers, and Meatloaf

Our culture holds up romantic love as the noblest of pursuits. We are led to believe that the need for romantic affection is built into every single one of us, so that we instinctively yearn for that tingly, bubbly feeling that we call "falling in love." We spend our lives in hopes of finding our soul mate — that one person out there just for us.*

The message to those who aren't dating someone is that you won't be content or complete unless you're in a relationship. It starts early. When my middle daughter was four years old, she watched a Disney movie about a prince and princess living happily ever after. When it was over, she asked me, "Daddy, who am I going to marry?" I told her she didn't need to worry about that right now and that I would make that decision when the time came. (Surprisingly, she seemed okay with that.) But the not-so-subtle message that she picked up on is that "if you don't have a prince, then you can't be a princess."

Christian bookstores aren't much better than our popular culture. Recently, I went to the section for single adults and found about twenty different titles. Seventeen of them dealt with finding your future mate. My favorite title was *If Men Are Like Buses, How*

---

*Since there are more women than men on the planet, statistically this is impossible. Besides if there was such a thing as a "soul mate" it would only take one person getting it wrong to ruin it for the rest of us. Just sayin'.

Can I Catch One? Again, the message is: You need to catch the bus and be in a relationship.

For many, romantic love becomes the focus of their lives. Pop music tells us that love makes the world go round and that all you need is love.* Pick your cliché, but what seems clear is that romantic love is the be-all and end-all. Nearly all of our music is about this kind of love, and it's been that way for a long time.

More than twenty years ago, the singer Meatloaf assured us that he'd do anything for love. The song remains popular today, thanks to commercials and the fact Meatloaf doesn't appear to have an expiration date, yet I've always puzzled that he'd do "anything for love," but the lyrics say he won't do "that." What does "that" refer to? Where does he draw the line? He won't share the TV remote control? Won't put down the toilet seat? Won't get rid of that unibrow? Did his girlfriend want him to change his name? That seems like a reasonable request from a potential Mrs. Loaf.

But the song raises a good question. Would you do anything for love?

If so, then romantic love has officially reached god status in your life.

Here's a thought that may surprise you: Life was never meant to be all about romantic love. Much of what we think of as romantic love was actually an invention of Western culture, something that didn't take hold until the Middle Ages. C. S. Lewis, one of the world's greatest classical scholars, wrote a study called *The Allegory of Love*. In it he explains how troubadours during medieval times popularized this hearts-and-flowers conception of love between a man and a woman. And it simply took hold of our part of the world and caused us to believe that the great purpose of life is the pursuit of an emotional, dramatic, passionate, romantic love.[30]

---

* At least it used to. Now it tells us to love somebody, get lucky, or simply says, "I need your love."

THE ULTIMATE NARCOTIC

Limerence. Psychologist Dorothy Tennov coined the term *limerence* in the 1970s after interviewing five hundred people about the love in their life. It refers to the phenomenon of falling madly, passionately in love, including what happens chemically in the body — including the powerful emotional attachment that comes over a person who is powerfully attracted to another person. Have you ever been "lovesick"?

It's an overpowering infatuation that involves "intrusive thinking" (not being able to concentrate on any subject but the object of our love); "putting the other on a pedestal"; agonizing over whether the feelings are reciprocated; fear of rejection; and some physical effects such as heart palpitations, loss of appetite, and paralyzing shyness around the object of affection.

Dopamine, the body's pleasure chemical, surges during limerence, so that love has a kind of stimulant effect. Energy increases. Appetite decreases. It's a blissful feeling, but a two-edged sword. Rejection can cause a dangerous crash. The increase in dopamine can bring about a decrease in serotonin, a chemical that helps us make wise decisions. This explains why people who are "head over heels" will do crazy, spontaneous things they would never ordinarily do.

Those who study limerence say that it burns itself out after eighteen to thirty-six months. At that point, if things have worked out for the couple, and the love is returned, then a deeper, more comfortable and less disruptive stage of love will result. The honeymoon, as they say, is over, but the marriage can begin.*

Limerence is a fairly new field of study, but it certainly offers its share of explanations for the sometimes wonderful, sometimes insane experience of romantic love.

---

* Frank Tallis, "Crazy for You," *The Psychologist* 18, no. 2 (February 2005): 72–74.

It's not as if romantic affection itself didn't exist before the Middle Ages. Reading the Song of Songs in your Bible will show you it did. But romantic love as the great quest, an obsession, something we must have or be miserable, is a more recent cultural invention. God has wired most of us for intimate fellowship, for a special mate, someone to complement us. But in modern times we've inflated that idea to crazy proportions. We look to romantic love as the secret to our satisfaction and the missing piece to make life feel complete.

It's love itself that becomes so attractive, once we've seen Edward run through the forest with Bella or Romeo come to Juliet's window. We want the hearts and the flowers, and we want our stories to end with the words "and they lived happily ever after."

Romantic love is a good thing, but when we make it essential to life then it becomes a false god. When we put our hope in romantic love and sacrifice for it, we have to ask if this beautiful gift from God has actually replaced him. When that happens the ending is rarely "happily ever after."

Looking for Love

In Genesis 29, we come to a love story that reads more like something from a reality TV show. It's *The Bachelor B.C.*

Jacob, Abraham's grandson, has left home and gone to visit a relative named Laban. When he gets there, he seems to almost immediately fall in love with Laban's daughter Rachel. "Now Laban had two daughters; the name of the older was Leah, and the name of the younger was Rachel. Leah had weak eyes, but Rachel had a lovely figure and was beautiful. Jacob was in love with Rachel and said, 'I'll work for you seven years in return for your younger daughter Rachel'" (Genesis 29:16 – 18).

Jacob was in love? What did he really know about Rachel at this point? Mostly that she had a lovely figure and was beautiful. But he had it bad for her and makes a deal with her father that he'll work seven years for her hand in marriage. That's a significant sacrifice he's willing to lay down on the altar of romantic love.

When my wife and I were dating, I took her to see a show called "Stars on Ice." She enjoys watching ice-skating. She loves the costumes, the music, the graceful movement. I remember sitting there watching the skaters come out in their little outfits and dance around on the ice. I hated every second of it. I knew I would, but I still bought the tickets and made time in my schedule to take her. We've now been married for eighteen years and my wife knows that the only way we're going to watch people skate on ice is if they're wearing pads and carrying large sticks.

As much as I hate to admit it, that's not the total truth. My wife would only need to bat her eyes at me and I would be more than happy to give up some money and time to take her to see an ice-skating show. Why? Because I would do anything for love, even that.*

What we sacrifice the most for has the most potential to become a God replacement. Jacob loves Rachel but doesn't have any real romantic interest in Leah. Leah is described as having "weak" eyes. That doesn't mean that she couldn't see well or required thick, horn-rimmed glasses. It contrasts Leah's appearance with that of her sister. It's possible that having "weak" eyes is meant to be a compliment. But if you have a friend who is setting you up with a girl and you ask "What does she look like?" you know you're in trouble if the answer is, "Well, she has weak eyes."

Jacob works for seven years to get Rachel as his wife, and in Genesis 29:20 we read an incredibly romantic verse: "So Jacob served seven years to get Rachel, but they seemed like only a few days to him because of his love for her." That is so sweet. In the

---

* And she has a lovely figure and is beautiful. (This footnote was added after she read the first draft of the book. Please don't tell her I added this. But if you decide to tell her I added this, please don't tell her I told you not to tell her.)

next verse, Jacob says to Laban, "Give me my wife. My time is completed, and I want to make love to her."

Okay. That's not quite as sweet. Probably wouldn't find that verse in a Hallmark card. But seven years is a long time to wait.

To make a long story short, they hold a feast. Laban probably plies his new son-in-law with wine. Jacob stumbles to his tent, and they send in his wife — according to tradition — for the marriage to be consummated. But the next morning Jacob wakes up, rolls over, and finds a pair of weak eyes staring back at him. He thought he was marrying Rachel but somehow ended up marrying Leah.

I know what you're thinking: *How did that happen?* I'm not sure, but my guess is Jacob was really drunk and it was really dark and he didn't realize it was Leah until the light of day. It sounds like a bad Jerry Springer show.

Jacob quickly sobers up, stumbles into his pants, and runs out of the tent looking for his father-in-law. He's no doubt furious. Laban seeks to renegotiate the deal and tells Jacob that he can have Rachel as his wife as well but it will cost him another seven years of labor. Jacob has no choice but to go along with the new deal. Now he has two wives and one big mess. But it's not Jacob I really feel sorry for in this story. It's Leah. Leah really loves her husband. She would do anything for him to love her back. She undoubtedly feels incomplete without her husband's love and affection.

A New Love

Over the years it's Leah, not Rachel, who gives her husband plenty of children. If you read through the names of her children, they tell the story of the disappointment and heartache she experiences in her love life.

Leah names her first son Reuben, for "the Lord has seen my misery. Surely my husband will love me now" (Genesis 29:32). She has a second son and says, "Because the Lord heard that I am not loved, he gave me this one too." With the third son, she says, "Now at last my husband will become attached to me, because I have borne him three sons."

With each son she has, Leah thinks maybe now her husband will love her. But with each child she is left disappointed. For years Leah puts her hope in romantic love, but she continues to feel the pain of rejection and loneliness.

But then, in verse 35, there is a compelling twist. "She conceived again, and when she gave birth to a son she said, 'This time I will praise the Lord.' So she named him Judah. Then she stopped having children" (Genesis 29:35).

"This time I will praise the Lord." Leah is taking her husband off the throne of her heart and giving God his seat. This time she puts her hope not in her husband, but in the Lord. How many times has the god of romance left you brokenhearted? Maybe this time you should praise the Lord.

The name she chooses, Judah, is a play on the Hebrew word for praise. And if we turn to the beginning of the book of Matthew, we see the family tree of Jesus. Here's what it says: "Jacob was the father of Judah." It's not Jacob's son Joseph or Benjamin, his two favorites by Rachel, that are referenced. Instead it's Judah, the fourth son of a switcheroo wife. Judah, the commemoration of a moment when a woman turned her eyes back to God.

Like Leah, most of us have learned that when we experience rejection from someone that we care about, it can be painful.

A friend of mine was recently giving me some frequently used breakup lines and describing the way the person being broken up with hears them. For example:

- When one person says, "I want to date around," the other person hears, "I want to see if I can find someone better."
- When one person says, "Let's just be friends," the other person hears, "Don't ever contact me again."

- When one person says, "You are too good for me," what the other person hears is, "I'm too good for you."
- When one person says, "It's not you; it's me," what the other person hears is, "It's not me; it's you."

The examples were funny, until he got to one I had been on the receiving end of.

Leah chose to find her identity, value, and hope in the love of God. It took the rejection of a man to help her realize the power and contentment that comes from God's love and acceptance.

Yes, love makes the world go round. In a sense, the Beatles were right — all you need is love. But it's a different love than most people expect. All we need is the love of God. He is the only one who can fill the void. When we feel that deep pang of loneliness, that's God crying out within us for fellowship. He wants to give us the love we have sought in all the wrong places.

The void in the human heart is God-shaped, not boyfriend- or girlfriend-shaped.

No Mistake

Looking back, Shannon could never remember pursuing God. What was clear was that God pursued her.

In her junior year she met a teacher who was a dedicated follower of Christ. He let Shannon know that he was praying for her, and this led to conversations about God.

There was a spiritual void in her life, and she knew it. "I need something," she told him. "I need something in my life." So he told her what it meant to find ultimate love and acceptance in Jesus Christ. "Come to church with my wife and me," he said. "We'll save you a place."

One Sunday she decided to test it out. She drove across town and found that even though she hadn't told them she was coming, the couple was waiting for her in the back row with a seat saved for her. It felt amazing to be cared about this way. Afterward, at home, she cried out to God. "I don't know if you're real," she prayed. "I don't know if I accept all this stuff or not. But I need you! I need something!"

Shannon became a Christian, and she reached out to the church. For her the church turned out to be God's hospital, where her wounds could be healed. She heard his voice saying to her what he says to you as well: "You are not a mistake! I make no mistakes. In you I made a beautiful child whom I love passionately, completely, and eternally. Come to my arms and feel the forgiveness that is a forever thing. I have the love and tenderness you have always sought. I have the healing that your soul deeply needs."

As Shannon surrendered her life fully to God, she discovered that God had other blessings in store. She knew beyond any shadow of doubt that Jesus completed her. The love and acceptance of Christ was enough, but then God brought Brian into her life.

Shannon and Brian dated for two-and-a-half years, during which they agreed to abstain from physical affection. Handholding and hugs were the limit. Brian understood that Shannon was working things out, and he was fine with this arrangement. "I just want to be with you," he said.

She found how sweet, how enriching the relationship between a man and a woman can be when they are bound by the love and worship of the true God.

To hear Shannon tell more of her story, go to zndr.vn/QMvgeZ.

Idol ID

Are you disappointed with your guy/guy relationships?
Do you find that your life is somehow not complete if you're not dating someone?

If you are dating someone, do you find that your boyfriend or girlfriend is constantly disappointing you? Do you find yourself wondering if maybe the problem is that you're simply dating the wrong person and your soul mate is still out there somewhere? And that the issues you're facing will go away once you find him or her?

How you answer those questions reveals where you've put your hope. And where you put your hope answers the question of what god you really worship.

Who do you sacrifice the most for?

Most of us could tell a story or two of how we've sacrificed to show our love to someone we had romantic feelings for. Certainly, God calls us to love selflessly and sacrificially in our relationships. But how do those sacrifices compare to the sacrifices you make in your relationship with God? Have you ever changed your appearance or your values to fit in with your boyfriend or girlfriend?

Think of an altar that represents your relationship with God. What are the sacrifices you've laid on that altar out of love for him?

Who is it that completes you?

When we look to someone other than God to complete us and define our lives, it's idolatry. It's also never works, because God is the only one who can complete us. We are made for him. In the future you may discover that a relationship with a spouse is a wonderful and precious gift, but it was never meant to replace a relationship with the giver of life.

CHOOSING JESUS:

Jesus My Identity

Idols are defeated not by being removed
but by being replaced.

The god of romance came in and swept us off our feet. We fell head over heels. The music was playing. Our hearts were pounding. Our palms were sweating. Life was like a really corny romantic comedy.

We were in love with love, with the idea of a "soul mate," someone custom-made for us. The two of us would create our own world and lock out everyone else. We would complete each other's sentences, laugh at each other's jokes, and stare into one another's eyes.

But something went wrong. Once the giddiness wore off, we discovered that human beings are human. They fall miserably short of being God. When we look to someone to be our god, they are going to let us down. When we say to someone, "I want you to satisfy me; I want you to save me; I want you to be my source of significance," what we're really saying is, "I want you to be god to me."

No human being, we discovered, can meet all our needs. No human being deserves that much pressure. But Jesus can do it—Jesus our identity. It was wonderfully liberating to break free of the shackles of romantic love and discover what it meant to be truly loved. Jesus once said that no one has greater love than the one who will lay down his life for a friend. And then he proved it.

the god
of relationships

An epic battle rages in space and on a nearby moon between the Galactic Empire and the Rebel Alliance. Spaceships, star cruisers, Death Stars, and X-wings fight for the future of the universe. But inside the Death Star, there's a battle for Luke Skywalker's soul. Will he turn to the "dark side"? Will he be tempted to follow the same path as his father?

As the young rebel leader walks into a large, dark room, the evil Emperor Palpatine turns in his throne and says, "Welcome, young Skywalker, I have been expecting you."

Palpatine seems to know everything that's going on — the attack by rebel forces, the fight at the shield generator on Endor. It's as if he can see into the future.

"I assure you, we are quite safe from your friends here," he says.

Luke looks worried, but he calmly responds, "Your overconfidence is your weakness."

The emperor immediately hisses back, "Your faith in your friends is yours."

This climactic scene from the classic movie *Return of the Jedi* is filled with action, emotion, and awesome special effects. It's science fiction at its best. But although it's a work of fiction, Palpatine speaks some truth. For a lot of us, our faith in our friends is our greatest weakness. We trust our friends and put our greatest hope in earthly relationships. We seek to please and fit in with our friends, even when it goes against what we know God would want.

Just like other false gods that push their way into our hearts, the god of relationships looks harmless — even Christian — at first glance. After all, when Jesus was asked about the greatest commandment, he said to "Love your neighbor as yourself" (Matthew 22:39). Of course, that was the *second* part of this verse. The first and greatest commandment is to "Love the Lord your God with all your heart and with all your soul and with all your mind."

Picture it this way: Your life is a bicycle wheel. Every spoke in the wheel represents different and significant relationships that make up your life. One spoke represents your mom. One spoke represents your dad. One spoke represents a sibling. One spoke represents your future spouse. Other spokes represent future children. Then there are different spokes for various friends, and on it goes. Our tendency is to make God a spoke in the wheel. But God isn't interested in being another spoke in the wheel of your life. God wants to be the center hub that all the spokes come from and connect to.

Our relationship to the Father is basic to who we are and to why we have been created. We are intended to love our parents, siblings, friends, and family members wholeheartedly — but always in the context of our primary, foundational love for God. Worship is for God alone. He must be our deepest love — actually the source of every other love. For only when we love God properly can we begin to love others properly.

According to the Ten Commandments, we are to *honor* our parents. But we are to *worship* only the Lord God. That's what you might call a "top button" truth.

Buttoned Up

Sometimes I'm in a hurry in the morning, and I button my shirt all wrong. Has this ever happened to you? Like most people, I take it from the top. Except sometimes in my rush, I choose the wrong slot to push that top button through. I usually don't recognize my mistake until I get to the bottom and figure out everything is out of line. But if you get the top button right, then everything else falls into place.

God has ordered our lives so that devotion to him is the top button. If that relationship is in proper order, then you're going to find that every other relationship, whether family or friend, falls into place in a far more satisfying way. But if you're wrong on him, you'll get everything else wrong too.

Augustine, an early Christian leader and writer, called the false gods in our lives "disordered loves." He knew legitimate objects of love could fall into disorder, just like a misbuttoned shirt.

It's precisely because a child should love a parent, a parent should love a child, and friends should love each other that these relationships can be elevated to false gods. We're doing what we're supposed to be doing. We simply go too far and don't realize we've gotten things out of order.

"But I can't love my family and friends any less," you might say. No, you can't, nor is that the message of this chapter. But you can love them differently. You can love them in the context of your primary devotion to God. And that, you will find, turns out to be a far greater, healthier, and more fruitful love.

The Test

One of the most harrowing stories in all of Scripture is found in Genesis 22. The story of Abraham and Isaac asks us this question: What if we were asked to prove that our love and commitment to God is greater than anything or anyone?

Abraham was a crucial figure in the history of humanity. God promised him in Genesis 15 that his offspring would be as numerous as the stars. Just one problem — he and his wife Sarah didn't have any children. But the Bible says that Abraham believed God's promise. He would be the first of a new nation, a nation that would be used by God to bless the world.

After the promise is made, nothing happens for a long time. Then when Abraham is one hundred years old, Sarah gives birth to Isaac. So it must've been a huge surprise to Abraham in Genesis 22:2 that God says, "Take your son, your only son, whom you love — Isaac — and go to the region of Moriah. Sacrifice him there as a burnt offering on a mountain I will show you."

"Your only son, whom you love." It's fascinating to me that this is the first time in the Bible the word *love* is used. The context is a beloved son who must be offered up as a sacrifice. That, of course, will become the theme of the Bible itself. The unity in God's Word never ceases to amaze me.

No parent in the world can hear the story of Abraham and Isaac without trembling. As someone in Isaac's age group, you probably shudder a little as well. In stories, we become the characters. We identify with them. And in this one, Abraham and Isaac are Bible heroes no one wants to be.

But we need to extend the parameters of this story. The more beautiful a relationship is, the more capacity it has to become an idol. Who do you love so fiercely, so protectively, so desperately? For whom would you lay down your life? A younger sibling? A parent? Your best friend?

I suspect there's some person or thing in your life that fits that description — a gift that is the test. If not, a day will come when you'll feel that way about a relationship.

Verse 3 tells us that early the next morning, Abraham sets off for the very place where God sent him. If he struggles, if he debates within himself, he doesn't do so for long. He is up with the sunrise, preparing his mule, preparing his heart.

After a couple of days, they can see Mount Moriah in the distance, and Abraham tells the servants, "We will worship and then we will come back to you" (Genesis 22:5).

Don't miss that word — *worship*. This is a meaningful point in the story. The presence of the word worship, at the moment of truth, tells us everything about Abraham's heart. In choosing God over everyone else, he is defining what it means to worship.

The other word that stands out is *we*. "We will worship and then *we* will come back to you," Abraham says. But how exactly will "we" come back if he plans to sacrifice his son? In the New Testament, we read that Abraham believed that God would raise his son from the dead. It's clear that he still fully trusts God. After all, God has promised a nation through this son.

A lot is made of Abraham's faith, but what about Isaac's? He's not stupid. He knows his dad has been acting a little strangely. But he trusts his father and God enough to follow Abraham up the mountain.

The Bible tells us that they walked on together, and after a while, Isaac says, "Father?"

"Yes, my son?"

"The fire and wood are here, but where is the lamb for the burnt offering?"

"God himself will provide the lamb for the burnt offering, my son."

And they continue to walk, until they come to the place God has described. Abraham builds the altar and arranges the wood. Then we can only wonder about the emotions as Isaac lets his father bind him and place him where the sacrificial animal should be. Because let's face it, Isaac could've gotten away. Experts believe Isaac was in his late teens or early twenties, so he could've easily bested his hundred-plus-year-old father in a footrace or wrestling match.

The account doesn't go into feelings; it deals only with firm obedience. Abraham reaches for the knife. Isaac doesn't flinch.

As the knife descends, a voice from heaven stops Abraham in his tracks: "Do not lay a hand on the boy," he said. "Do not do anything to him. Now I know that you fear God, because you have not withheld from me your son, your only son" (Genesis 22:12).

WHO DO YOU LOVE?

In 2007, the Barna Group asked more than one thousand people to choose their most important relationship. Seven out of ten adults chose their earthly family over God.
Other findings:

- One out of three said their entire nuclear family is more important than God.
- Twenty-two percent named their spouse as the most important relationship in their lives.
- Seventeen percent placed their children in the top position.
- Three percent chose their parents.
- Only two percent named a specific friend as their most important relationship.
- Nineteen percent named God, Jesus Christ, the Trinity, or Allah as their top relationship. The most likely to make this designation were people over forty years in age.[*]

[*] Jennifer Riley, "Study: God Relationship Not Most Important to Americans," *Christian Post*, March 17, 2008, www.christianpost.com/news/study-god-relationship-not-most-important-to-americans–31548/ (accessed October 4, 2012).

Abraham passes his test. And Isaac looks pretty good in this story as well. Both showed a depth of commitment to God. God has never and will never require a human sacrifice as an act of worship, but I wonder how you or I would fare. I wonder about the depth of our worship, our commitment to God. If you had to choose between the gift and the giver, who wins?

Disordered Loves

If the story of Abraham and Isaac is a troubling narrative, so is Jesus' statement in Luke 14:26. It's one of those passages we don't talk about too often. Jesus says, "If anyone comes to me and does not hate father and mother, wife and children, brothers and sisters — yes, even their own life — such a person cannot be my disciple."

This is a great example of a verse that cannot be taken out of context. We know from the full counsel of Scripture that we are to love our families. One of the commandments explicitly tells us to honor our parents, and we know Jesus would never contradict God's law. So as we dig a little deeper, we discover that in Jewish culture, hate was used to express a lesser form of love. The New Living Translation gets the idea of this verse when it says, "You must hate everyone else by comparison."

So we're really not discussing a lack of love for people. We're discussing the centrality and the sheer magnitude of our love for God. A relationship of disordered love takes God's place in our hearts and is ultimately destructive to that relationship. Or to put it in the positive, we love others best when we love God most. Allow me to describe a few of the consequences of placing another human being on the throne of your heart.

Unreachable Expectations

You may feel the burden of living up to goals that your parents set, because the bar feels like it's out of reach. Are you the baseball player whose parents build their lives around your athletic accolades? Perhaps you're the bright daughter who could possibly earn a full scholarship to an elite university. Do you ever think, *It wouldn't bother me so much to make a B. But it would kill my parents. They live for my report cards.*

Those of us who counsel people see many adults who grew up believing they could never please their parents. Whatever they did, it was never enough. They are still trying to make their mom or dad proud by hitting a home run or bringing home a perfect report card. When parents place their value in their child, it puts the child in God's place in their lives. And that's a lot to ask, even for an honor-roll student.

Unreasonable Disappointment

A friend of mine used to read comic books when he was a boy. Ads offered X-ray glasses and sea monkeys — amazingly wonderful things — for only a buck or two. But he really wanted a set of a hundred army men that came in a cool heavy-duty chest. The picture in the comic book was awe-inspiring: a great trunk, brass-trimmed with padlocks, and packed with amazing toy soldiers in all kinds of fighting positions. He saved his two dollars and sent off for the army men.

Six weeks later a little package came in the mail — a paper box about two inches by four inches, filled with ant-sized toy soldiers made of paper-thin green plastic. All of them looked the same and would break if you looked at them wrong.

Even as a kid, he knew it was unreasonable to expect the amazing toy he visualized for only two dollars. Sometimes it's easier to understand that other things — money, pleasure, drugs — won't satisfy the soul. But relationships are different. We know God ordained them. We're made for community. It's the basis of society. So we tend to think we can create heaven simply by having great friends.

But the deepest joy can come from only one source. As wonderful as friends can be, we must know that they won't be perfect. They won't satisfy the soul. When we look to those relationships to do those things for us, we will inevitably be disappointed when the package is delivered.

Undeserved Criticism

My car ran out of gas a while back. I knew it was running low, yet I kept driving around, thinking prices would drop a penny or two if I held out. Eventually, the car wheezed to a stop. I climbed out seething with anger.

But I wasn't mad at myself, I was angry at my car. I slammed its door to let it know how I felt. I kicked its tire to express my disappointment. How could the car do this to me? I know that's ridiculous, but we all have our irrational moments. It's irrational to expect a car to do what it was never designed to do. It's just as irrational to become upset at someone else for failing to give us happiness and satisfaction that it's not in their power to give.

If I am constantly critical of others for the emptiness I feel or if I am always giving the ones I love a hard time for not meeting my needs, it's most likely because I'm asking them to do something they weren't made to do. They can give me love and happiness, but there's a deeper satisfaction and contentment that must come from God alone. Criticism often marks our families and relationships because we want someone to do for us what only God can do and they are always falling short.

On the Altar

We can't expect things or people to fill a God-shaped void. So how should we look at our family relationships? Should we love less? Of course not. But we should love differently.

Growing up, Jason Roy, the lead singer of the chart-topping band Building 429, idolized his dad. His parents divorced when he was five. When his mom remarried and moved from Texas to California, he went with her. But at fifteen, Jason decided he needed his father's influence and moved back to Texas.

"I thought I was moving in with my superhero," Jason says. "I mean, really, he was Superman incarnate."

When Jason fought with little boys on the playground, saying, "My dad is stronger than your dad," he meant it. Jason's dad took first place in his weight class at the Texas powerlifting championships two years in a row. He was a coal miner who worked all day at the coal power plant, then came home and went straight to the gym to lift for three hours. He drag raced on the weekends. He ate nails and spit out BB's.* This guy was larger than life. But when Jason moved in, he knew something wasn't right. Different drugs and different things made Jason's home life difficult and brought down the "dad idol" that Jason had built in his mind.

With one idol gone, Jason's faith in Christ began to grow and become his own.

"When I moved in, my father and my stepmother would be asleep on Sundays," Jason says. "I'd wake up and take my sister to church because my life was chaos at home.

"One of the reasons that I dove into my faith was because it was the only thing that was unchanging in my life. When I walked into the church, I was welcomed with open arms and treated with love and respect. People kept telling me about this love that would never fail and about a guy who would pursue me relentlessly. And the more that I dug into that, the more I was like, 'Well, that's what I want here on this earth.'"

Jason chased after the Lord, putting him firmly on the throne of his life. And over time, God healed his relationship with his father as well. His dad started listening to Jason's music and eventually returned to the roots of a faith that he'd had as a child.

"It's a really cool thing now," Jason says. "My dad and I have a great relationship, and only God could have reclaimed and ransomed that relationship for sure."[31]

---

*Not really. But he did have a blue ox named Babe.

Jason discovered that the supreme act of love is setting your heart on Christ. Doing that leads to the most loving relationships possible.

And oh, yes — there's a postscript to Abraham's story. It shows the poetry and symmetry of history, when we look at things from God's perspective. God had sent Abraham on a three-day journey to Mount Moriah with Isaac. That's quite a hike. Why would he do that?

After this story, one thousand years passed. According to 2 Chronicles 3, the king of Israel, David, bought a little acreage to build an altar and worship God. It was the place of Abraham's near sacrifice. On that property, Solomon built the great temple of Jerusalem. Another thousand years passed. On this land, once again, a Father sacrificed his Son. This time it was no test. "He who did not spare his own Son, but gave him up for us all — how will he not also, along with him, graciously give us all things?" (Romans 8:32).

What God asked of Abraham, but did not finally require, he was willing to do himself, for you and me. He had a choice. On one side was his own beloved Son, sinless and perfect. On the other sat you and me, entangled in all the sin that makes us unworthy of his blessing. The only way we could be reconciled was by way of a sacrifice. And God so loved the world that he gave his only Son.

You are asked to choose God, to make him the source of our worship. But know this: He has already chosen you.

Idol ID

What person or people matter most to you in this world?
This is not a question you need to discuss with others. Just between you, your reflections, and God — who is it that you love so much that you'd lay down your life for them?

Take a moment to compare the sacrifices you are willing to make for that person with the sacrifices you have made to follow Jesus. Can you tell a story of how you personally sacrificed out of your commitment and devotion to Christ?

Is there a relationship in your life that seems to be the determining factor in whether or not you are happy and joyful or sad and depressed?
To what extent does this person, or persons, determine your state of mind?

To what extent have you organized your life around this relationship?

It's worth comparing the emotions you experience in worship. Though worship can be a quieter and more introspective experience, can you say that you experience feelings that approach the depth of what you experience with your friends or family? Yeah, I know, it's a tough question.

The sources of our greatest and deepest emotional expression provide a strong clue to who or what controls us.

Can you find signs of "disordered love" in your relationships? How would a deeper worship of God affect these symptoms?
Review the effects of disordered love near the end of this chapter. Do you recognize these in your own relationships?

Imagine your life as a fully devoted worshiper of God and follower of Jesus Christ. Envision yourself laying your relationships at the altar, along with every other part of you. You tell God, "I can't do this right. I worship you and you alone, and I trust you to make me the son/daughter/

friend I need to be. I love these people deeply, but they will no longer be the meaning of my life. Only you will be. Help me be the person I need to be, so that you can bless these relationships. May these beautiful gifts from you make my heart more completely yours."

CHOOSING JESUS:

Jesus My Everything

Idols are defeated not by being removed
but by being replaced.

The god of relationships painted a beautiful picture. It showed a car full of friends, a yearbook full of signatures, a Facebook page filled with likes, a loving family. Parents, siblings, and grandparents were all there, and they clearly loved one another.

Who wouldn't respond to those things? It's what we all want. The god of relationships may have been the most deceiving of all the false gods, because he seemed so decent and proper. He offered something that is already one of God's greatest gifts. But he offered a distorted version of it.

What he offered was a facade, a place to shut out the world. He offered obsessive relationships, in which everyone must play god to someone else. He called all of it love, but in retrospect, it looked more like desperation. We followed our friends until we smothered them. We made demands of our parents until we exhausted them.

Jesus showed us what relationships were supposed to be. He helped us understand that all of the relationships inside the home, at school, and at church are reflections of what he is to us. It's the love of Christ that teaches us how to love each other. We said, "Relationships are everything," but it wasn't until Jesus was our everything that we discovered everything relationships can be.

the god
of me

I read a blog post the other day about a book published in 1964 called *The Three Christs of Ypsilanti*. The book was based on a psychiatric case study by Dr. Milton Rokeach, who was documenting mental illness.

Rokeach was treating three patients at a psychiatric facility in Ypsilanti, Michigan. These patients, named Leon, Clyde, and Joseph, all suffered from delusions of grandeur, a common disorder. However each of these three men believed that they were actually Jesus Christ. The doctor worked hard at the task of introducing them to reality, but it was difficult to break through. In his book he tells about trying to convince these men that they really weren't God in the flesh.

For several years he had these three guys live together. They ate all their meals together. They slept in the same room together. Every afternoon they had group therapy together. Dr. Rokeach hoped that spending time with others who thought they were God would help reality set in. His approach led to some interesting conversations.

One of the men would say, "I'm the Messiah, the Son of God. I was sent here to save the earth."

"How do you know?" Rokeach would ask.

"God told me," the patient would invariably answer.

But just then, another of the three would interject, "I never told you any such thing!" And once the third got into the act, there was chaos. Once the disagreements became sharp and angry, each "Christ" would merely assume that the other two were simply patients in a mental hospital. He, on the other hand, was the genuine article.

Sadly, Rokeach wasn't successful in his attempts to convince the men that they weren't God. They were trapped in this upside down reality where they thought they were the center of the universe and life was really all about them.

The foundation of reality is that there is one God, and you are not him. Once that's established, a choice must be made:

- I know that there is the Lord God, the master of all creation.
- I also know there's the god of me, the pretender to the throne.

Whom will you serve?

In my brokenness, I feel the pull to worship me. I hear the whispered lie that Adam and Eve first heard: "Your eyes will be opened, and you will be like God" (Genesis 3:5). Why serve? You rule! You have everything you need to be your own god. Every day is a trip to that orchard where the snake is waiting. I must face this same choice: Will I worship God, and find my true place in this universe, the perfect place he has arranged for me? Or will I worship me and decide I can somehow come up with a better life than the Creator of all could design?

It's no coincidence that we've left the god of me for last. You'll confront many of the gods in our lineup at some point in your life. But this is one you'll grapple with every single day — multiple times per day.

Recognizing the God of Me

There are some symptoms that start to show up when the god of me edges himself onto the throne of my heart.

One symptom is arrogance. I'm always right. My way is the best way. The god of me won't listen to the wisdom of others.

During a recent Christmas, we opened presents at my in-laws' house. I was putting together one of the kids' toys on the family room floor and my father-in-law was sitting in his recliner watching the hunting channel — the channel that sends the message, "My son-in-law will never be a real man because he doesn't shoot things or build things." I don't know if he was more amused by the TV show or by the sight of me trying to put something together. I could feel the pressure mounting as I tried desperately to screw in a screw. It wouldn't catch the threading. My father-in-law said, "I think that's a reverse screw." I took that to mean that it screws in the other way. I was sure he was making this up in an attempt to further expose my wimpiness in front of my other male relatives. I was not going to be fooled. I knew the saying "righty tighty, lefty loosey." It's not "righty loosey, lefty tighty." I kept turning this screw to the right, certain that there was no such thing as a reverse screw and too proud to take the advice of my father-in-law.*

So let me ask you this. When was the last time you made one of the following statements: "I was wrong," "You were right," "I should have listened to you," or "I like your idea better"? Even when we don't realize it, if saying those things is difficult, a touch of arrogance may be present in our lives.

Another symptom that surfaces when I start to worship the god of me is insecurity. The god of me is consumed with what others think and terrified of trying something and failing. You can't help but be self-conscious, because when you're god, it's all about you.

---

* My editor says I need to finish this story. Whatever. I don't have to if I don't want to.

How about defensiveness? Have you ever found yourself taking the slightest suggestion or the blandest criticism as a personal attack? What makes people this way? Well, when you're god, you must be perfect, and no one else could possibly be in a position to criticize you.

The god of me will make you lonely, because you can't handle equals. You certainly can't handle authority. You need people who constantly reaffirm that it's all about you.

Listen to what God says: "In the pride of your heart you say, 'I am a god; I sit on the throne of a god'... But you are a mere mortal and not a god, though you think you are as wise as a god" (Ezekiel 28:2). The god of me is the most relentless idol of them all.

Gods at war? It's really me versus God. It's the flesh versus the spirit. All the other gods, in one way or another, take God off the throne and put me in his place.

TUBES AND TEENS

What messages does TV teach? Is it to be helpful and kind? Or is it to look out for yourself? That's what a group of researchers from UCLA wanted to know. In 2011, they studied the last forty years of popular TV programs aimed at preteens. In the 1970s, 80s, and 90s, top-rated shows for kids highlighted themes such as: the importance of community, being kind to others, and tradition. Out of the sixteen values studied, fame ranked thirteenth or lower in every decade except the most recent one. Now fame is number one.

The predominant message of today's preteen shows seems to be that a successful life is all about finding a way to be famous.

"With Internet celebrities and reality TV stars everywhere, the pathway for nearly anyone to become famous, without a connection to hard work and skill, may seem easier than ever,"

---

one of the researchers said. "I was shocked, especially by the dramatic changes in the last ten years. If you believe that television reflects the culture, as I do, then American culture has changed drastically."*

---

* Stuart Wolpert, "Popular TV Shows Teach Children Fame Is Most Important Value, UCLA Psychologists Report," *UCLA Newsroom* (July 11, 2011), newsroom.ucla. edu/portal/ucla/popular-tv-shows-teach-children–210119.aspx (accessed October 20, 2013).

Broken Cisterns

It's an inescapable conclusion: Worshiping the god of me is not in my best interests. The god of me takes many forms, but none of them satisfy. There is an image that is used in Scripture that captures what happens when I put myself on the throne of my heart instead of God.

In the Old Testament book of Jeremiah, God speaks through the prophet Jeremiah and makes his case against his people. "'Therefore I bring charges against you again,' declares the Lord.... 'My people have exchanged their glorious God for worthless idols. Be appalled at this, you heavens, and shudder with great horror,' declares the Lord. 'My people have committed two sins: They have forsaken me, the spring of living water, and have dug their own cisterns, broken cisterns that cannot hold water'" (Jeremiah 2:9, 11 – 13).

He summarizes their rebellion into two sins: They have rejected him and have instead turned to worthless idols. He explains to the people that when we put ourselves on the throne instead of God, it's like digging our own broken cisterns to drink out of when there is a spring of fresh, living water flowing right beside us.

Cisterns were an important part of everyday life in Israel during Jeremiah's time. In fact thousands of them have been uncovered by archaeologists. Rain was infrequent and scarce about half the year, so the people in those days would dig cisterns and line them with bricks and plaster to hold the water. But cisterns were always breaking and losing water. Even when they didn't break, the water would often become stagnant or the supply would be inadequate.

The people would have thought of Jeremiah's metaphor was ridiculous. No one would ever choose a cistern as his water source when a spring of crystal clear water was available. But that captures the ridiculousness of idolatry. We choose a broken well with stagnant water, instead of the spring of fresh water. We look to something or someone to do for us what God was meant to do for us.

Instead of looking to God as a source of comfort, we turn to mindless entertainment.

Instead of looking to God as our source of significance, we turn to our accomplishments.

Instead of looking to God as a source of security, we look to what we can do to make our futures more certain and comfortable.

Instead of looking to God as our source of joy, we look to our family, friends, or boyfriend or girlfriend.

Instead of looking to God as our source of truth, we look to popular opinion, entertainment, and what teachers and those in authority tell us.

The things we look to for help aren't necessarily bad or evil in and of themselves. In fact, God may use them to accomplish his purpose, but the questions are: *Have they become broken cisterns that we turn to instead of the living water? Am I putting my hope in something that doesn't hold water?*

A New Hope

Over the summer my family house-sat for some friends while they were out of town. It had been miserably hot and we were excited about using the above-ground pool in their backyard.

The second morning we were there my wife woke me up and

said the water level in the pool seemed a little bit low. She wondered if there might be a small leak. I went out to investigate. It was clear that the pool was slowly losing water. I got in the pool and put on my son's goggles. They were quickly cutting off the circulation to my head, so I knew I needed to find the leak fast. Eventually I located a hole about the size of a pencil eraser where the water was slowly leaking out.

I went to a pool store down the road and asked what I should do. They sold me an underwater patch for the pool and explained how to use it. It seemed simple enough. When I got back to the house, I followed the instructions. I applied the heavy-duty glue to the patch, put on the goggles, and swam down to apply the patch. When I started to press the patch against the side of the pool, I watched in horror as the tiny hole slowly started to expand to the size of a basketball. Suddenly eighteen thousand gallons of water rushed out and tried to push me through this hole.

I fought my way against the current and got out. In a panic I grabbed towels and tried to stuff them in the hole. The hole just got bigger. Finally I came to the realization that there was nothing I could do. I stood there in teeny goggles and watched helplessly as all the water emptied out of the pool into the backyard. My kids came out with stunned and disappointed looks on their faces. My youngest had tears in his eyes. One of my daughters looked at me and said what I was thinking: "Did that really just happen?"

That's a moment many of us have experienced, metaphorically speaking. This is the inevitable moment of truth when you worship the god of me in all its forms. You watch all the water come rushing out and, though you try desperately to contain it, there isn't anything you can do.

That's how some of you feel about your relationships. You have a best friend that you're sure will be faithful and honest to you. You put your hope in that person. But you've been patching one leak after another, making compromises, and it seems as if all the water is running out of that friendship. With panic and dread you look on, but it seems like there is nothing you can do.

The god of me, in all its forms, always leaves you disappointed and disillusioned. So here's the question we're left with: Is there another hope? In Romans, Paul speaks of a hope that doesn't disappoint.

God longs for you to experience his living water. As he tells Jeremiah, the heavens look on with great horror at the sight of God's children drinking from the nasty cisterns and rejecting the fresh living water. It's one of the most heartbreaking things for God the Father to watch. He has provided for and given his children what is pure and life-giving, and they reject it. Guys, imagine it this way (girls, you're going to have to imagine even harder): You're going to your first prom and take your date to eat at Ruth's Chris Steak House. She orders the filet mignon. It's brought to the table on a sizzling plate. Done to perfection. You can't help but smile. Sure, the steak cost you nearly fifty bucks, but it's going to make the night extra special. But then imagine that when it's time to eat, your date reaches into her purse and pulls out a piece of unwrapped, half-eaten beef jerky. It's got some mold on it as well as some lint. Right in front of her is a perfect filet, and she is chewing old beef jerky. How would you respond? You would get upset. You've paid for the steak. This date is supposed to be special. You want her to experience the best. You would be both frustrated and saddened at the same time.

That's how God feels when he sees his children reject his water for their own stagnant cisterns.

The Living Water

The "Living Water" is a title that Jesus gave himself in John 4. Jesus is traveling when the Bible tells us he "had to go through Samaria." If you look on a map, that doesn't seem entirely accurate. He didn't really have to go through Samaria. There were certainly ways around it. And most Jews would have done whatever necessary to stay out of Samaria, because of the prejudice between the two peoples. But John says that Jesus had to go through.

A woman lived there who had been desperately searching for something or someone to put her hope in, but time and again she had watched all the water rush out. Her search always ended in disappointment.

When Jesus arrives in Samaria, he comes to a well. A well is different from a cistern. A cistern collects rainwater. A well allows you to draw water from underground. But as with cisterns, getting water from a well required a lot of effort. And like cisterns, wells would often dry out or be full of stagnant water.

It's about noon when Jesus shows up at this well. It's the heat of the day, and Jesus is no doubt tired from walking. He sits down to rest at the well. He's thirsty, but there isn't much he can do about it because the well is likely around a hundred feet deep and he has no way to draw water from it. His disciples head off to grab some lunch at a nearby village but Jesus stays behind. He knew this woman would be coming soon.

When she arrives at the well to get water, Jesus says to her, "Would you give me a drink?" She does a double take and asks, "Why is it that you, being a Jew, would even speak to me?" And Jesus says to her, "If you knew who I was, you'd ask me for water" (John 4:7 – 10, my paraphrase).

My guess is that at this point she thinks the sun must be getting to this guy. She points out to Jesus that he doesn't even have a bucket with which to draw the water. Jesus explains to her that if she drinks his water she'll never be thirsty again. He has something that will satisfy her thirst forever. She is thinking in terms of the physical world, that Jesus has physical water to quench her physical thirst. She has nothing to lose and so she agrees to drink this magical water from this strange stranger.

Jesus tells her to go back home and get her husband and then come back. She tells him that she doesn't have a husband. Then Jesus, with a gentle smile, says, "You've spoken the truth. You've had five husbands and the man you're living with now is not your husband."

She realizes he's some kind of prophet and immediately tries to take the spotlight off of her by changing the subject. She asks a theological question. Jesus quickly answers it but she still doesn't understand. So she says in verse 25, "I know that Messiah (called Christ) is coming. When he comes, he will explain everything to us." She says to Jesus, "I know when Christ comes he'll makes sense out of things."

Then in verse 26 Jesus says to her, "I, the one speaking to you — I am he." This is the only time we know of in his entire life that Jesus voluntarily revealed his identity. Imagine this moment for the woman. Her search had finally come to an end. Five husbands, that's five different cisterns, and all of them leaked. None of them held water for long. But when Jesus reveals who he is, there is something within her that knows he is the one her soul has been longing for.

What Jesus says to this woman he also says to you and to me. "The water I give...will become in them a spring of water welling up to eternal life" (John 4:14).

So what are you thirsty for? Are you stressed out and thirsty for peace? Are you lonely and thirsty for love? Are you bored and thirsty for purpose? Are you thirsty for acceptance? For validation? For significance? Are you just thirsty for something more? The god of me relentlessly calls us to chase after all these things. But ultimately we're left more thirsty than ever.

After the woman at the well believed in Jesus, she became the well woman. The Lord's invitation is the same to you: "Drink from me, and you'll never thirst again."

Idol ID

Do you find it difficult to say "please" or "thank you"?
You may need to ask your friends or family for their opinion. The god of me often blinds us to our own self-absorbed behavior. After all, if you're a god, people *should* do things for you. We're entitled to preferential treatment. If this idol is running your life, you probably don't utter thankful words too often.

Do you find yourself complaining a lot?
If you just heard the family car got in an accident while your mom was driving, would you immediately think, *How does this affect me?*

Okay, you might think about your mom first, but if your second thought was immediately about yourself and if you'd still have a car to drive, it provides a big clue as to who's on the throne of your life. Complaining people can easily be caught up in the world of *me*.

When you see your best friend, do you ask about their day or immediately start talking about yourself?
Do you always choose what movie you're going to? What place you'll eat at? What snack to buy? We're all pretty fascinating people — you, me, our friends and family. Do you really get to know the people in your life? If we're stuck in shallow relationships, it may because we're stuck on ourselves.

CHOOSING JESUS:

Jesus My Lord

Idols are defeated not by being removed
but by being replaced.

The god of me attacked at our weakest point—ourselves. We believed life should be all about me. The word idolatry looks the way it does for a reason, because it starts with "I" and rhymes with *me*. This god said we should "Look out for number one," "Take care of ourselves," and "Build our self-esteem." It promised throngs of adoring friends, tons of talent, and fame beyond belief.

But when you live on an island with the emphasis on the *I*, it quickly becomes a lonely place. Friends leave, fame fades, talents go unnoticed. Instead of loving ourselves, we end up hating how self-absorbed we've become. If we're the lord of our lives, we'll soon become a slave to our own selfish desires.

No human—not even ourselves—can make us truly happy. Then Jesus came. The apostle Paul said, "If you declare with your mouth, 'Jesus is Lord,' and believe in your heart that God raised him from the dead, you will be saved." Jesus saves us from our sins and from ourselves. He meets our deepest needs. When we put him on the throne of our life and ourselves in the proper place of worship, it frees us to live with ultimate joy and power.

idol winner

"The human heart is an idol factory. Every one of us from our mother's womb is an expert in inventing idols."
— John Calvin

Imagine this: Your father, the king, is dead. He had only reigned two years — two long, evil years. He put up idols and worshiped false gods. He ruled to please himself. His officials finally had enough and assassinated him in the palace. The people rejoiced. That's what you'd think, but they didn't. Instead, they killed those who killed your dad and put you in his position. Talk about a dysfunctional nation.

So now you're the king. Oh, and did I mention the fact that you're only eight years old? Ruling an unruly nation is no job for a child, yet you handle it masterfully. Your grandfather and your father were known for their evil deeds. You turn things around.

You probably already recognize that this isn't an imaginary story. This is the reality that King Josiah lived. So we're talking about good kings, bad kings, and downright evil kings. But the Bible tells us that Josiah, "did what was right in the eyes of the LORD and followed completely the ways of his father David, not turning aside to the right or to the left" (2 Kings 22:2).

Instead of following the idols that his father, Amon, and grandfather, Manasseh, erected, Josiah turned back to the one true God. When Josiah took the throne, the nation of Judah was filled with beautiful shrines to false gods, while the temple of the Lord was filled with idols and falling apart. When he was twenty-six, he ordered that the temple be repaired. As workers rebuilt God's house, they discovered the Book of the Law. Josiah called all the people together to hear the word of the Lord. When they heard the power and promises of the one true God, they dedicated themselves to follow him, and Josiah took the lead. He broke down shrines and pulled down altars. He smashed the false gods into tiny bits — literally.

Josiah knew there was only room in his nation, his people, and his heart for the one true God.

Heart of Worship

Josiah not only led his people in destroying all other gods in their lives, he also showed them how to worship. Since God first led his people out of Egypt, the Israelites had celebrated Passover. But in the eighteenth year of Josiah's reign, the king put on a Passover to end all other Passovers. Talk about a party!

He provided thirty thousand sheep and goats and three thousand cattle as Passover offerings. Musicians played and the people ate, danced, and celebrated for seven days. Second Chronicles 35:18 says, "The Passover had not been observed like this in Israel since the days of the prophet Samuel; and none of the kings of Israel had ever celebrated such a Passover as did Josiah."

The king gave away much of his material wealth to celebrate God. In our modern thinking, many people associate worship with religion. We think worship has something to do with robes, rituals, and really old music. If someone doesn't have a drawer in the dresser of their life labeled "organized religion," then they assume that the question of what god they worship doesn't apply to them. They might have drawers labeled "school," "family," "money," and "hobbies," but not "worship."

The problem, of course, is they misunderstand what worship is.

As a member of the human race, they are by definition worshipers. It's factory-installed, standard equipment — not a buyer's option. Every action, every word, every thought is an act of worship to something or someone.

When you subtract the religious language, worship is the built-in human reflex to put your hope in something or someone and then chase after it. The end result, of course, is that our lives begin to take the shape of what we care about most. The object of your worship will determine your future and define your life. It's the one choice that all other choices are motivated by.

Josiah chose to worship God with his possessions, his words, his actions, and his heart. And God blessed him for his decision.

Ideal Idol

If someone ever asks you, "What's so special about Christianity? What sets it apart from Buddhism, Hinduism, Islam, or anything else?" your answer is found throughout the Bible. The main storyline that runs through God's Word shows his pursuit of people.

God is imagined in countless ways on this planet. Maybe he lives on Mount Olympus, as the Greeks thought, and comes to earth only when he's bored. Maybe "he" is actually an entire pantheon of gods, as the Hindus have it. Maybe there are so many of them that you need a scorecard to keep track. Maybe God is just another word for nature, as the pantheists believe, meaning that the tree outside my window is God; this chair is God; hey, you and I are God! Maybe there is no God as a separate being, as the Buddhists have it; the answers are supposedly within us.

Christianity offers a view of God that is strikingly different from any other. In Christianity, there is one God. He is all-powerful. He takes an active role as Father to every human being. His most striking feature is not anger or power or transcendence or even creativity, but instead is his relentless, all-consuming love. No one would have made up such a God. The idea is too outrageous.

This is a God who comes from heaven, from all of his perfection and purity and might, to us, in all of our weakness and impurity. He puts on skin, taking the form of a helpless baby all in pursuit of your heart. This is God who, when turned down, ignored, rejected — even violently, even blasphemously — finds a new way to express his love and issue the invitation. This is a God who has never given up on winning your heart. Never.

Josiah understood that God was the ideal idol, because he's not an idol at all. Josiah's father and grandfather put up idols, he chopped them down and pointed people to a God who is close to his people. The God who's the Creator of all, the Master of the universe, the Father to the fatherless, the King of all Nations. Second Kings 23:25 says, "Neither before nor after Josiah was there a king like him who turned to the Lord as he did — with all his heart and with all his soul and with all his strength, in accordance with all the Law of Moses."

With all his heart and with all his soul and with all his strength, you've heard that before in this book. Here's something else you've read a lot: "Idols are defeated not by being removed but by being replaced." Josiah removed a lot of idols and was celebrated for his devotion to God, but the battle for his heart never stopped. False gods don't give up easily, and Josiah discovered that.

At the end of 2 Chronicles, it says Pharaoh Necho from Egypt went to Carchemish to fight the Babylonians. But to get there, the Egyptians had to pass through Judah. Instead of letting him pass through, King Josiah disguised himself and went out to meet Necho in battle.

Why did Josiah decide to fight when Necho said there was no quarrel between their nations? Necho even said that God had told him to hurry to battle (2 Chronicles 35:21). The Bible doesn't answer this question. Maybe the god of achievement was whispering in Josiah's ear, "You've done so much, but wouldn't it be a huge feather in your cap to defeat the Egyptians?" Maybe the god of me was saying, "You don't need God to do this. You're powerful enough on your own."

We don't know why Josiah marched out to meet Necho in battle, but we do know the results. Josiah was shot with an arrow and died in Jerusalem. What a sad way for a great king to die. All of Judah and Jerusalem mourned for him.

Fighting the false gods of this age is a life-long battle. Every day is filled with decisions. Don't just win the battle for your heart —win the war.

notes

1. Michael Kell, "10 Commandment Video Survey." YouTube, YouTube, LLC. April 15, 2008. Web, www.youtube.com/watch?v=yrO9LKGEbEk (accessed October 20, 2013).

2. "Americans Know Big Macs Better Than 10 Commandments," Reuters-Life!, New York. October 7, 2007, www.reuters.com/article/2007/10/12/us-bible-commandments-idUSN1223894020071012 (accessed October 20, 2013).

3. Tim Challies, *The Next Story: Life and Faith after the Digital Explosion* (Grand Rapids: Zondervan, 2011), 184.

4. Erwin Lutzer, *Managing Your Emotions* (Wheaton, IL: Victor Books, 1988), 109.

5. Michael Jordan and Mark Vancil, *Driven from Within* (New York: Atria, 2005), 110.

6. Paul Copan, *Is God a Moral Monster? Making Sense of the Old Testament God* (Grand Rapids: Baker Books, 2011), 35.

7. Paul Thompson, "'My Body Is Only for My Husband': U.S. Christian Model Kylie Bisutti Quit Victoria's Secret Because It Clashed with Her Faith," *Daily Mail*, February 8, 2012, www.dailymail.co.uk/femail/article-2097793/Kylie-Bisutti-quit-Victorias-Secret-clashed-Christian-faith.html (accessed September 28, 2012).

8. Edward F. Murphy, *Handbook for Spiritual Warfare* (Nashville: Thomas Nelson, 1996), 239.

9. *Nelson's New Illustrated Bible Dictionary*, ed. Ronald F. Youngblood, F. F. Bruce, and R. K. Harrison (Nashville: Thomas Nelson, 1995).

10. Gordon J. Wenham, *Genesis 1 – 15* (Waco, TX: Word, 1987), 226.

11. "Transcript: Tom Brady, Part 3," CBS News, *60 Minutes*, February 11, 2009, www.cbsnews.com/2100 – 18560_162 – 1015331.html (accessed June 11, 2012).

12. Derek Abma, "Men Think of Sex Only 19 Times a Day, Report Finds," *Vancouver Sun*, November 30, 2011.

13. M. Scott Vance, *The Chronicle of Higher Education*, quoted in *Christianity Today* 29, no. 18 (December 1, 1997).

14. "The Impact of Video Gaming and Facebook Addiction," Anti Essays, www.antiessays.com/free-essays/130731.html (accessed March 18, 2012).

15. Martin Lindstrom, *Brandwashed* (New York: Crown Business, 2011), 71 – 73.

16. Masuma Ahuja, "Teens Are Spending More Time Consuming Media On Mobile Devices," *The Washington Post*, March 13, 2013, articles.washing tonpost.com/2013 – 03 – 13/news/37675597_1_teens-cellphones-video-games (accessed October 21, 2013).

17. Winifred Gallagher, *New: Understanding Our Need for Novelty and Change* (New York: Penguin, 2011), 126.

18. Robert J. Morgan, *Nelson's Complete Book of Stories, Illustrations, and Quotes* (Nashville: Thomas Nelson, 2000), 545.

19. C. S. Lewis, *Mere Christianity* (1952; San Francisco: HarperSanFrancisco, 2001), 135 – 36.

20. Constance Rhodes, *Life Inside the Thin Cage: A Personal Look into the Hidden World of the Chronic Dieter* (New York: Random House, Shaw Books 2003), 5 – 6.

21. Annie-Rose Strasser, "Eighth Grader Gets Seventeen to Stop Photoshopping the Girls in Its Magazine," July 3, 2012, thinkprogress.org/media/2012/07/03/510564/eighth-grader-gets-seventeen-to-stop-photoshopping-the-girls-in-its-magazine/ (accessed October 21. 2013).

22. Tatiana Siegel, "Hollywood and Steroids: When A-List Actors Go the A-Rod Route," *The Hollywood Reporter*, August 22, 2013, www.hollywoodreporter.com/news/hollywood-steroid-use-a-list – 609091 (accessed October 21, 2013).

23. Rhodes, *Life Inside the Thin Cage*, 204.

24. Eric Quiñones, "Link Between Income and Happiness Is Mainly an Illusion," Princeton University, June 29, 2006, www.princeton.edu/main/news/archive/S15/15/09S18/ (accessed October 21, 2013).

25. Jere Longman, "Drugs in Sports, An Athlete's Dangerous Experiment," *The New York Times*, November 26, 2003, www.nytimes.com/2003/11/26/sports/drugs-in-sports-an-athlete-s-dangerous-experiment.html?page wanted=all&src=pm (accessed October 21, 2013).

26. Thomas J. DeLong, "Why Chronic Comparing Spells Career Poison," CNN Money, June 20, 2011, management.fortune.cnn.com/2011/06/20/why-chronic-comparing-spells-career-poison/ (accessed October 2, 2012).

27. Tony Campolo, *Who Switched the Price Tags?* (Nashville: Thomas Nelson, 2008), 26 – 27.

28. Longman, "Drugs in Sports, An Athlete's Dangerous Experiment."

29. "Real Stories," Taylor Hooton Foundation, www.taylorhooton.org/real-stories/ (accessed October 21, 2013).

30. See C. S. Lewis, *The Allegory of Love: A Study in Medieval Tradition* (Oxford, England: Clarendon, 1936).

31. Phone interview between Jesse Florea and Jason Roy on September 13, 2013.

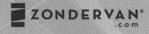